THE WORLD BEYOND

THE WORLD BEYOND

A Novel of Ancient Greece

DEANNA MADDEN

ISBN-10: 0692897739
ISBN-13: 978-0692897737

Cover design by SelfPubBookCovers.com/diversepixel

Flying Dutchman Press

2017

For Doug and Gypsy

.

I declare
that later on,
even in an age unlike our own,
someone will remember who we are.

—Sappho

Mighty indeed are the marks and monuments of our empire
which we have left. Future ages will marvel at us, as our
present age marvels at us now.

—Thucydides, from Pericles' Funeral Oration

429 B.C.

CHAPTER 1

They say ships can see the glint of her gold-tipped spear as they approach land. I wouldn't know since I've never been on a ship, but she is always the first thing I notice when I step through the high columned gateway that opens onto the Acropolis. There she stands, larger than life, wrought in bronze, Athena Promachos, protectress of the city, looking every bit the fierce warrior goddess she is in her helmet and breastplate with her slender spear upthrust against the backdrop of the clear blue sky.

Seeing her gives me courage to approach the marble pillared temple where the Great Goddess stands like a colossus in her inner sanctum, jeweled eyes staring blindly, shield by her side, winged Victory perched in the palm of her hand, the most magnificent statue in this city of statues, dwarfing all others in comparison. My fingers tremble as I press an offering of honey cake into the claw-like hands of her priestess, a crone with sunbaked skin and obsidian eyes who stands mutely beside the stone altar. Through the pillars I can glimpse the goddess, but I dare go no closer. To step into her presence is an act of great temerity, and I don't wish to anger her. Closing my eyes, I whisper my prayer. *Great Goddess, be merciful. Take pity on an orphan who has neither mother nor father nor brother to protect her. Let me remain unwed a little longer. I am in no hurry to be a wife and mother.*

I would continue, but my old nurse Zobia tugs impatiently at my arm and others press forward, eager for their chance to supplicate the goddess, so reluctantly I turn away and we descend the temple stairs. Retracing our steps, we pass between the tall columns of the Great Gateway and start back down the stair, surrounded by the horde of citizens and slaves who like us have climbed to the citadel to pay homage to the gods or consult with the guardians of the state.

I don't have much confidence that the goddess will help me when so many others are clamoring for her aid. Our city is under siege, and we are dying from a plague. In the face of so much calamity, why should she concern herself with my problems? They must seem hardly worth her notice. Not that she is noticing the bigger problems either. For a long time she has been deaf to our cries and pleas for help.

In the agora people whisper that Athena has forsaken us, that we are being punished for offending the gods with our war against Sparta. They say the gods have turned their backs on us and favor Sparta now, and if Sparta wins, it will trample Athens and her citizens in the dust. It will be the end of our city and all her glory. The Spartans will tear down the beautiful buildings we have built and defile our sacred places. I can't believe Athena will allow that to happen. We are her people; every child in the city knows the story of how she chose us and gave us the olive tree as a sign of her favor. When the Persian hordes invaded, she protected us. Surely she will again.

Meanwhile, the war drags on. We are in our second year now, and our temples have become refuges for people from the countryside seeking shelter within the city walls while the Spartan army burns their homes and crops. And as if being besieged were not bad enough, now the gods have sent this plague that kills as ruthlessly as the swords of our enemies. Day and night the priests burn offerings, but still the pestilence creeps like a blight across the city, claiming old and young alike.

It took my brother Jason in late summer, my mother two weeks later, and then my father a short month ago, leaving me alone in this world. After my father's funeral rites, my uncle Lycurgus took me in and rented our house to a family of refugees. Zobia, who has watched over me since infancy, came with me, but the other household slaves were sold because my aunt and uncle have no use for them.

They hoped I would be like a daughter to my Aunt Damaris, who yearned for a daughter as well as a son. But with little skill at the loom or the distaff and no interest in learning to manage a household or cook, I've been a disappointment to her. I'd rather curl up with a scroll of poetry, which now I can do only in stolen moments or I'll hear again how my father should never have taught me to read. "What could he have been thinking?" my aunt repeatedly laments. "It will be a wonder if any man wants to marry you."

At this I sigh and roll my eyes, but I know better than to contradict her. She will only scold me more if I tell her I have no interest in marrying. But unfortunately finding a husband for me has become her goal now that the thirty days of mourning have passed. I think I'm still too young for marriage, but she insists fifteen isn't too young. Was she not a mere fourteen when she wed my uncle Lycurgus? To wait longer is to tempt fate, she tells me. For if I reach the age of twenty unwed, who will want me then? As if it matters when people around us are dying of plague and Sparta's army is threatening Attica. If things go on like this, I may be dead or enslaved before I turn twenty, so what difference does it make if I have a husband or not? A husband won't save me from slavery if Athens falls.

But these arguments do not sway my aunt, which is why I climbed the great stone stair to the Acropolis with my old nurse today and appealed to Athena for help. I know my aunt won't approve when she hears of our outing, but I'm desperate. I told myself maybe she wouldn't notice that we were gone. Of course that was wishful thinking. I might as well be the nymph Io trying to escape the hundred-eyed giant Argos. The whole house knows the minute we walk through the door. We are greeted by a cry from Myrrine as she carries a stack of bowls to the dining room.

"Where have you been?" she demands, exasperation in her voice. "Your aunt's been asking for you this past half hour. You'd better go to her at once."

At twenty Myrrine is not married, but then she's a slave and has no choice in the matter. At least she has not become bitter or resigned like so many slave women, and she is still pretty with brown hair escaping in wisps about her face and smooth olive skin. I like her, but I wish she would not always treat me like I'm ten.

"Well, don't just stand there," says Zobia, giving me a gentle nudge. "Run. See what your aunt wants."

I slip my sandals off with a sigh and bound upstairs. I know exactly where my aunt will be — in the north room at her loom, the sun slanting in through the narrow windows and striping the yellow tiles on the floor. I have lived under her roof only a month, but my feet know the way as well as if I grew up within these walls.

"Ah, there you are," my aunt says as I burst into the room. Her brow is knitted in concentration as her hands dart with practiced skill among the threads stretched taut on her loom, eyes never wavering from the shuttle. Her jet black hair is caught back in a neat chignon and she wears a long violet tunic that brings out the color of her eyes. "Where have you been, child?" she says without breaking her concentration. "I've asked half a dozen times and they said you were nowhere to be found."

"I went to the Parthenon," I answer and brace for a scolding.

Her frown deepens. "You went out without telling me?"

I hang my head, trying to look contrite. "I knew you wouldn't approve."

"Then why did you do it?"

I hesitate. But I have resolved to tell the truth. "To make an offering to Athena."

Her eyes dart to my face. "It's no excuse. You have no business running about like a girl of the lower classes or a common slave. What will people think? Besides, it's not safe out there. There are all sorts of beggars, thieves, and lowlifes in the city now. Decent women stay at home, where they belong."

"Zobia was with me," I say, glad now that I took my old nurse along. My first plan was to go alone. It was not as if I didn't know my way to the Great Stair. I have walked it before in the Panathenaic processions when the girls of the city wear garlands of flowers and carry Athena's new robe to her singing songs of praise as they go.

But my aunt dismisses this with a wave of her hand. "It makes no difference. What use would an old woman be if you ran into trouble?"

I sigh. Arguing with her is useless. For my aunt her house is all the space she needs. Within its mud-brick and plaster walls she is in charge now that Lycurgus's mother, old Xantippe, is in her dotage. There is nothing outside she wants. She has her family, her loom, her servants, her house. What does she care about what happens in the rest of the city? The beautiful temples on the Acropolis could be razed and it would make no difference to her. The statues of heroes that line the Street of Statues could be toppled and she wouldn't care. Mobs could riot in the streets and it wouldn't faze her — unless they broke into her house.

But I am different. For me the city calls like a siren song. The narrow winding streets, the Acropolis with its Great Stair and magnificent gateway, the marble temples, the crowded agora, the gymnasiums, the amphitheater where the play competitions are held, and a hundred other places — there is so much to see and do. I should have been born a boy. Then no one would have thought twice when I walked out the door. My brother Jason often left the house and no one questioned his right to go where he chose. Who knew where he was? At the gymnasium wrestling? Outside the city walls horseback riding with his friends? Practicing javelin throwing at the stadium? Sometimes he took me with him to the agora. My mother and father did not forbid it. When we returned, there were no recriminations. "Did you have a nice day?" my mother would ask while she was braiding my hair.

No, she was nothing like my aunt. A lively and curious woman, she always seemed to know what was happening in the city. She loved to go to festivals and could play the lyre and sing. Her high sweet voice could bring tears to your eyes and her laughter could warm the hardest heart. I miss her so! My father too, who was as different from my uncle as my mother was from my aunt. Where my father was gentle and undemanding, my uncle Lycurgus is stern and uncompromising. Where my father had progressive ideas, my uncle is a slave to convention. Could there be two brothers more unlike?

But my aunt and uncle were kind to take me in after my family died of the plague, as Zobia frequently reminds me. It's ungrateful of me to compare them in my mind.

My aunt's voice pulls me back to the present moment. "Once you are married, there will be an end to this roaming. A husband will keep you at home and soon enough a woman's duties."

Inwardly I groan. She means of course *children*. I know only too well how children can weigh a woman down. I've seen it often enough in the homes of relatives. Even with the help of slaves, children require their mother's time and energy. They have to be fed, taught, cajoled, entertained, and disciplined. It's endless and exhausting work. And that's if you're fortunate enough to survive childbirth. No, I'm in no rush to be a mother.

"As a matter of fact," says my aunt, "I think we've found a husband for you."

My stomach sinks. "*What*?"

"In fact, if we're lucky, you might be married before the end of the year."

"Who?" I manage to gasp in a barely audible whisper. I feel as if I am deep under the sea and no words, only bubbles of air, can escape from my mouth.

My aunt doesn't seem to notice my distress. She continues to push her shuttle across the loom with practiced skill. I think if the earth shook under the city at this moment, she would still push her shuttle across just so. "I doubt you know him. Euphrastus, son of Linus. His family owns shares in the silver mines at Laurium. He rents out workers to the city."

My heart plummets. No, I don't know him, but I feel certain he is a short fat bald man with hairy arms and sweaty palms. He'll be at least fifteen years older than I, if not more, as most men don't marry before they have completed military service. I think with a shudder of cousins older than I wed to men twice their age who order them about like slaves or ignore them. Is that to be my fate? *Athena, are you listening?*

"Must it be so soon?" I try to fight down the tidal wave

of panic rising within me. There must be something I can say to change her mind.

"Your mother would have wanted this," my aunt insists. "We must do our duty as your nearest kin to see that you're taken care of."

I doubt my mother would have wanted to rush me into marriage, or my father either. They would have let me wait a little longer and they would not have wed me to a man who makes money renting out slaves to the city, but I don't say this. I hear Zobia's voice in my head warning me to mind my tongue. Perhaps I'm being unfair. Perhaps Euphrastus, son of Linus, isn't as dreadful as I fear. I wait for my aunt to dismiss me and then fly back downstairs in search of Zobia to find out what she knows about this proposed match.

CHAPTER 2

I find Zobia with Myrrine in the courtyard tending the cooking pot. They are cutting up onions and leeks under a blue sky while the smoke from the brazier rises.

"You mustn't blame me if you got a scolding," Zobia says as I rush up out of breath. "I told you your aunt wouldn't approve of that climb to the Acropolis, but would you listen? Oh no, I could talk myself blue and it would make no difference."

"I don't care if she scolds me," I retort and peer into the pot to see how the soup is coming. The steam from the pot and the heat from the fire make me take a step back, but the aroma of simmering soup has already set my mouth watering. Climbing the Acropolis has made me hungry.

"We're eating early," Myrrine informs me. "Your uncle's having a banquet later."

"Again?" It seems as if my uncle holds banquets at least once a week. My father didn't hold nearly so many.

"It's not your place to judge," Zobia admonishes me. "It's men's business."

She always says this when I question my uncle's routine.

"You'd think they'd be concerned about catching the plague," I mutter.

"Hush. You'll bring bad luck down on us." She spits to ward off evil.

"I'm sure no one sick is invited," murmurs Myrrine, stirring the soup in the pot. She is young and mention of the plague doesn't frighten her as it does Zobia.

It occurs to me that my prospective husband may be among the guests. "Who's invited?"

"Why the sudden interest?" Zobia asks suspiciously. "Why do you care who attends your uncle's banquet?"

"No reason." I try to look disinterested.

"Then why do you ask?"

Since Zobia has known me all my life, I can seldom hide anything from her. She can read me like a scroll, that is, if she could read.

I abandon my effort to appear disinterested. "Have you heard of Euphrastus, son of Linus?"

Zobia furrows her brow in thought. "Is he a poet?" She asks this because she knows my love of poetry.

I groan. "No, he rents out slaves."

"Since when are you interested in such things?" Myrrine wipes her forearm across her damp forehead. Cooking is hot, sweaty work.

"Since my aunt told me I might soon have to marry him."

Zobia and Myrrine exchange a quick look that tells me

this does not come as a surprise. I can't believe it. Why is it that I'm always the last to know, even when something concerns me deeply?

"You knew about this?" I demand, shocked that they didn't warn me.

"No," Zobia says, adding more onion to the soup, "but I'm not surprised. Your aunt has made no secret of her desire to find a husband for you."

This is true. I can hardly blame them for what is common knowledge in the household. "Well, do you know who he is?" I ask again.

Zobia shakes her head and Myrrine avoids my eyes. I stare at Myrrine, willing her to look up. There's something she's not telling me.

"Athens is full of men," she says, tossing another leek into the pot. "Am I supposed to know them all?"

"I don't want to get married," I say through gritted teeth.

Zobia sighs. "It doesn't matter what you want. You'll have to do what your aunt and uncle decide."

I know she's right, but I still don't like it. "I'll bet he's short and fat. I bet he snores and has a mother who rules his home with an iron fist."

"Maybe he won't be that bad." Zobia pats my arm. "And once you've given him a son or two, he may leave you alone."

I glare at her. This is no comfort.

"Just be grateful you're not a slave," Myrrine adds.

At this I feel a twinge of guilt. She's right. I shouldn't complain. My lot is better than theirs. Every Greek knows it's better to be freeborn than to be a slave. No doubt Myrrine would change places with me in an instant if given the chance. All the same, she doesn't have to worry about being married off to a total stranger.

I'm about to point this out when my cousin Nikomedes appears in the doorway. He's nearly as tall as I am although he's two years younger, and he has dark hair that is forever falling in his eyes. "What's for dinner?" he asks as he does every afternoon when he arrives home from school. He must think about food all day since these are invariably the first words out of his mouth. The answer is almost always fish or soup, but he never seems to tire of asking.

"Soup," I tell him. "We're eating light. Your father's throwing a dinner banquet later. Again."

"Right," he says and then disappears back inside, his curiosity sated.

It occurs to me that he may know something about the man his parents are arranging for me to marry. At any rate it's worth a try to ask him. Abandoning Myrrine and Zobia, I go in search of my cousin. I find him sitting on a couch in the hallway pawing through his schoolbag.

"Do you know Euphrastus, son of Linus?" I ask, getting straight to the point.

He scowls at his schoolbag and pulls out a tablet and stylus. "Should I?"

"I don't know. I thought you might since your father knows him."

"I don't know everyone my father knows."

Of course he doesn't. I hadn't meant to imply that he did, but it's not worth explaining. Disappointed, I turn to go back to the courtyard.

"He owns close to a hundred slaves," says a deep voice from the doorway that leads to the banquet room. Kalchas, Nikomedes' dark-skinnned pedagogue from Lydia, is standing there. He never says much and moves as silently as a cat. With his coal black eyes and brooding silence you never know what he's thinking. But evidently my aunt and uncle consider him trustworthy or he wouldn't be Nikomedes' pedagogue.

"Do you know him?" I ask.

Kalchas' eyes always make me uneasy. He looks like a man with secrets, very dark ones.

"No," he says, then without another word stretches out on a couch, hands behind his head, and closes his eyes. Conversation done. As usual, a man of few words.

"Why are you so keen to know who he is?" asks Nikomedes, curious now. "If my father knows him, can't you just ask him?"

"It's not that simple," I say, regretting that I brought up Euphrastus. What if Nikomedes or Kalchas tells my uncle that I have been asking questions about him? He might not like it. "Please don't tell him I was asking," I add hastily.

"Of course not," Nikomedes says. "He never listens to me anyway."

"I'm sure that's not true."

My cousin shrugs, unconcerned. He has no idea what it's like to lose a father. I hope he never does.

He looks up at me through a lock of hair that has fallen into his eyes. "You want me to find out something about him?"

I hesitate, tempted, then shake my head. It's not a good

idea to have Nikomedes trying to ferret out information for me. He's a nice boy, but after all, he's only thirteen years old. I shouldn't have mentioned Euphrastus to him in the first place.

"Are you in love with him?" Nikomedes asks, narrowing his eyes.

I feel the blood rush to my face. "No, of course not. I don't even know him."

"So why do you want to know?"

It's not a question I want to answer, but now I'll have to if I don't want him going around telling people I'm in love with Euphrastus. "Because I might have to marry him."

He frowns, considering this. "He might be at Father's banquet tonight. Want me to see if I can find out?"

Again I hesitate, knowing I should probably not get Nikomedes involved. Yet his offer is tempting. I want to know what I'm up against and who else can I ask? I glance at Kalchas, prone on the next couch, eyes closed. Is he listening? I can't tell. I decide to throw caution to the wind. "All right."

CHAPTER 3

Once I know that Euphrastus is coming to my uncle's banquet, I'm determined to catch a glimpse of him. How I'm going to accomplish this I don't know. The women of the house will be upstairs in the women's quarters while the banquet is underway since it's not proper for respectable women to attend. Of course there will be female slaves like Myrrine to take the men their food and drink, but I can't pretend to be a serving woman when my uncle is present. He'd have a fit. No, I have to find another way.

By now I'm familiar with the routine of my uncle's banquets. My father's banquets were far less lavish since he had less money than my uncle to spend on entertainers and food. My uncle's parties have something of a reputation. There is always a juggler, an acrobat, or a pretty boy who can play the lyre and sing, or flute girls, and of course hetairas—educated women, usually foreign, paid to make witty conversation and provide female companionship for these sometimes raucous events.

I could steal downstairs after my uncle's guests have drunk several rounds of wine. Standing in the doorway, I could glance quickly around the banquet room at the men lounging at their tables. Maybe I could spot the man my uncle wants me to marry, then steal away again without being observed. But since I have no idea what he looks like, what is the likelihood that I'll figure out which one he is? No, it's too risky. Someone is bound to notice me, and if I'm caught, my uncle will be furious. So far I have managed to avoid a beating since coming to live under his roof, but if I go too far, I have no doubt he will let me feel the smart of his cane. He's a man who believes in discipline.

In the end since I can't think of a way to safely spy on my uncle's guests, I beg Myrrine to spy for me.

"You have to let me know what he looks like," I tell her. "Just keep your eyes and ears open. I'll be forever grateful."

She rolls her eyes. "What does it matter what he looks like? You have to marry him if your aunt and uncle say so. He could have two heads and it wouldn't matter."

"Please!" I beg, desperate. "I'll give you my tortoiseshell comb."

Maybe it is the comb which convinces her, or maybe she takes pity on me. In any case she finally agrees. Then comes the long wait.

As the guests begin to arrive, my aunt Damaris and some of the women slaves retreat to the loom room, along with a sulky Nikomedes, who is not being allowed to attend the banquet because his mother thinks he's too young. I plead a stomachache so I can pass the time reading by oil lamp in the small room I share with Zobia while I wait for Myrrine. Reading is the only way I stay sane now that I live with my aunt and uncle. I live for the moments when I can take one of my precious scrolls from the little chest I brought with me from home and indulge in my favorite pastime — reading the poems of Sappho or a canto of Homer. However, on this night I am distracted by the noise from the banquet that drifts in through the open balcony door — a mingling of men's deep voices, the laughter of women, and music. My attention keeps straying from the words on the scroll before me, a poem by Sappho about Apollo's longing for the river nymph Daphne. He's trying to persuade her to stop running from him when Myrrine glides into my room and puts a finger to her lips to warn me not to speak. But I've already been waiting for an hour, and I'm dying to know what she has to report.

"Well, did you see him?" I keep my voice low. We both know it's best not to be overheard in this house of many ears.

She kneels beside me smelling of honey and wine and tucks back a lock of hair that has fallen across my cheek. "Yes, he's there. A man who prefers his wine unwatered. And he downed a platter of eels all by himself." She grimaces. A proper Greek never drinks his wine unwatered and downing a platter of eels all by himself suggests a lack of moderation. Neither are good signs.

"Is he short and fat?" I ask.

She shakes her head. "No, he's tall and he still has the build of a soldier. I'd bet he trains at the gymnasium. So you see, he's not as bad as you thought. Now I've got to go back before I'm missed."

"But you've hardly told me anything," I protest, clutching her arm. "What about your promise?"

She hesitates, as if holding something back. "He has a scar — here." She traces an invisible line down the left side of her face with her finger.

I shiver. It seems a bad omen. How did he get a scar on his face? Was it a war wound or did he get it in a fight?

"Now I have to go." Gently she disengages herself.

"Try to find out how he got the scar," I entreat her.

She rolls her eyes, then slips out of the room as noiselessly as she entered.

When she's gone, I set aside my scroll and walk out on the little balcony. Overhead there's a full moon in the sky. I know I have to be careful not to be seen by any of the men from the banquet who might wander into the courtyard. The women of the household are supposed to be invisible on these occasions. My uncle would not be happy if I broke this rule.

I stand there a while listening to the babble of voices rising from below. Then to my surprise a girl steps into the courtyard. She has light brown hair and wears a pink ankle-length tunic that glows in the moonlight, making her look like a sprite.

Curious, I lean over the parapet for a better look. A flute girl, I decide. She's too young to be a hetaira. Somebody's slave, rented out for a few obols, maybe part of an ensemble. I wonder, is it really so bad to be a flute girl? Surely it's more fun to listen to the conversation of men and make music than to be confined to the women's quarters.

She lifts a wood flute to her mouth and blows a few mournful notes that linger plaintively in the night air. They are haunting and beautiful, as if she has given the night a voice.

I must have made a sound because suddenly she looks up, her face a pale oval in the moonlight.

"Who's there?" she calls out.

Instinctively I draw back into the shadows. But then it occurs to me that she's only a flute girl, so what does it matter if she sees me? Emboldened, I lean over the parapet again.

"Oh, there you are," she says, looking up at me. "I thought I heard someone."

"Shh, they'll hear you," I warn.

"Lean out more so I can see you better."

It seems rude to refuse, so I lean out farther. "Please play some more," I beg her.

She blows a dozen quick silvery notes and then stops. "Who are you then — daughter of the house or slave?"

"Neither. It's my uncle's house."

"Are you the one who's to marry?"

My spirits sink. Am I a topic of conversation at the banquet as they pass the wine? The thought makes me cringe. "They say I'm to marry Euphrastus, son of Linus."

She puts her flute to her lips and blows a few notes of commiseration that so perfectly catch my feeling that I laugh.

"Is he so bad?"

"Would you like to see him?"

I hesitate. Suppose he's truly awful. Perhaps it would be

better not to know. But, no, the Greek blood flowing in my veins insists that it's better to know, even if the truth is worse than I can imagine. I gather my courage. "Yes!"

"All right. Stay there."

She disappears back inside. I strain my ears, but the voices from the banquet mingle indistinguishably. In a few minutes she returns, this time with a hulking brute of a man in tow. I catch my breath. Can this be the man my aunt and uncle intend for me to marry? The moonlight shines on the bald dome of his head. And what of his face? I won't get a good view of it unless he looks up, but if he does, he may see me. I can tell from the clumsy way he moves that he's drunk. He lunges at the flute girl, who deftly eludes him, as if she has had much practice dodging the advances of drunken men. I watch, my heart in my throat, hoping he won't catch her. In the moonlight she looks like a nymph or a dryad threatened by an ungainly bear. He's even worse than I feared. There's something about him that makes my blood run cold.

"So why did you drag me out here, you little minx?" he demands gruffly.

"To look at the moon," the girl says sweetly, turning her eyes upward.

He looks up and I see stern features, a cruel mouth, narrow eyes, and an ugly scar that runs down the side of his face just as Myrrine described. I press my fist to my mouth to keep from crying out. Is this to be my husband, a man who looks like a thief? No, worse. A murderer. How can my uncle give me to such a man? Does he want me to be miserable for the rest of my life? I can't believe he would be so heartless. My mind races. Perhaps I can reason with him. Perhaps if I promise to learn to cook or spend more time in the loom room? But somehow I don't think these things will make any difference. In fact, arguing may just steel him in his resolve. He has a stubborn streak. I've seen it several times since coming to live with my aunt and uncle. Once his mind is made up, it's difficult to change it. I'd probably be wasting my breath.

"I didn't come out here to look at the moon," Euphrastus growls.

"I'll play you a song then," the girl says, and lifting her flute to her lips, she trills a rush of notes that breaks off as she dodges another lunge. Laughing, she darts back into the safety of the lighted room, and he stumbles after her.

I wait to see if they will reappear. The minutes slip by. I strain my ears to hear the sound of the flute or the gruff voice of Euphrastus, anything that will tell me she is safe. There is only the same babble of voices as before. I listen to it for a while, but I might as well be listening to a foreign tongue. I can understand nothing of what they say. I'm about to give up and go back inside when two men step into the courtyard. I stay, careful to keep in the shadows on my balcony. They are about my uncle's age, but I can't see them well, just the tops of their heads and the gleam of their white robes in the moonlight. One is tall, the other short and stout.

"I'll wager Aegisthes will leave the others in the dust," the tall one says.

"My money's on Doros," says the other.

"I hear he's fast, but do you think he can beat Aegisthes?"

"I saw him at the gymnasium the other day. He's a handsome fellow, and there's not much he can't do."

"Oh, without doubt he's favored by the gods. Apollo himself would envy that body and face."

"The sculptors will be begging him to pose soon enough."

"True, and I dare say his pedagogue is hard pressed to beat off his admirers."

"Well, soon enough he'll have a chance to show his mettle. Pretty or not, he'll have to fight in this cursed war."

"Maybe it'll be over soon."

"I doubt that. The Spartans are just as determined on their side as Pericles is on ours. Neither side is eager for peace unless they can claim victory. No, this could go on for a very long time. Our children could still be fighting the Spartans when we are old men."

"I hope you're wrong but you may be right. It's a bad business—and now this infernal plague. At least the Spartans have had the good sense to keep their distance from our walls."

"Did you hear one of Pericles' sons has it?"

"No! Well, some would say the gods are punishing him."

"They are indeed. Well, life is short and none of us knows how long we have."

"You speak the truth, my friend. These are uncertain times."

"Let's go back in, pour a libation to the gods, and drink a toast to good health."

"Not politics?"

"By no means. I'm quite fed up with politics. I say send the politicians out to fight the Spartans. They got us into this mess."

Still talking, they drift back inside and the courtyard is empty again. I retreat to my room, thinking about what I have heard. Right now the plague seems less frightening to me than having to marry the cruel-looking man with the scar on his face. I don't want to marry anyone, but if I have to marry, why couldn't it be a young man, someone like the young Apollo they mentioned — Doros, an athlete who will compete in the coming races. If only someone like that could be the husband I'm destined to marry instead of the drunken lout I saw in the courtyard.

I sigh, pick up my scroll, and begin to read again. Apollo pursues and Daphne runs. I have read it countless times, but my heartbeat quickens. I am Daphne fleeing through the wood, Apollo hot on my heels. Her panic is mine. Never mind that he is a god. Once caught, she will never be the same. My pulse races. The sounds of the banquet recede. My lamp is nearly out of oil when Zobia comes in. The women have left the loom room and retired to their rooms, although downstairs the banquet continues.

"Still reading? You'll wear your eyes out, child. Put that away and go to bed."

Carefully I roll up the scroll and replace it in my chest with the other scrolls I brought from home. "Why do my uncle and aunt want me to marry this man Euphrastus?" I ask her.

"They want to see you happy with a husband and children of your own," she says as she unties her belt and sits down on her bed.

"I won't be happy married to him," I say, watching as she lets down her iron-grey hair.

"How do you know that? Are you an oracle? Can you see the future?"

"No, but I saw him tonight in the courtyard."

She looks at me, alarmed. "Did he see you?"

"No, of course not. I stayed in the shadows."

"Well, you'd better not let your uncle know. He won't be pleased."

I stretch lazily. "If I told him I don't want to marry Euphrastus, do you think it would make a difference?"

"No, I don't, Little One," she says, resorting to the old nickname that always makes me feel like a child but is comforting too. "It isn't your place to question what your uncle does."

"But I'll die if I have to marry him. He's horrible." If she had seen him in the courtyard tonight with the flute girl as I did, I think she would agree.

"You won't die," she says patiently. "You'll do what you have to do. Women don't choose their husbands."

I know this but I'm not ready to let the matter drop. "Why Euphrastus? Of all the men in this city, why him? I have a dowry. Surely my uncle could have found someone less unsavory."

Zobia sighs and comes to sit beside me on the narrow bed. She lowers her voice so no one on the other side of the wall will hear. "It's only gossip of course, but they say your uncle owes him money."

I stare at her. My uncle is rich. "How is that possible?"

She looks away. "Even rich people have debts."

"What do you mean?"

"They say he lost a wager."

"But surely—" I spring to my feet and begin to pace, as I'm wont to do when I'm agitated.

"That's what I overheard downstairs," Zobia says as she shuffles back to her own bed. "I probably shouldn't have told you, but there it is. Now be a good girl and go to bed."

"I'm to be given away like a slave to pay a debt?" How can she sit there so calmly? Why isn't she as upset as I am?

"There's nothing you can do. You'll have to accept your fate, as must we all. Now come give your old nurse a kiss, then put out the lamp and let's try to sleep. Banquet or not, we'll have to be up with the dawn."

I know this is true, and so I kiss Zobia on her weathered cheek, then lie down with a heavy heart on my own narrow bed and try to ignore the voices and laughter from the banquet below. Soon she is snoring, but I lie awake thinking. I miss my family and except for Zobia the world seems an uncaring and lonely place.

CHAPTER 4

When I wake in the morning, I remember that an unhappy future awaits me and groan. How could the gods be so cruel? Why has Athena not answered my plea? Why have I been spared by the plague only to find myself faced with a fate worse than death? Well, maybe not worse than death, but close to it. I know I'm being ungrateful and self-centered. The goddess has more important matters to concern herself with than who I will marry. I understand. There's a war going on. All over Athens people are falling ill and dying from the plague. Why should she bother herself with me, an insignificant girl? But then I think of Euphrastus, son of Linus, and I feel sick in the pit of my stomach. I don't want to marry a man uglier than Hephaestus. There must be some way I can change my aunt and uncle's minds.

Suppose I go to my Aunt Damaris and beg her to intercede with my uncle for me. Wouldn't he listen to her?

Maybe, if I could get her to do it. But chances are she will just scold me for my rebellious nature and lecture me on a woman's duties. I think I will gag if I have to listen to one more lecture about a woman's duties. Isn't it obvious to everyone that I'm not really cut out for the role of wife, mother, and household manager?

At last I give up trying to think of a way out of my dilemma and go down for breakfast. Not surprisingly, my uncle is still sleeping. The slaves tiptoe about and whisper in an effort not to disturb him. No one wants to be blamed for waking the master of the house. After a night of indulging, he is likely to be in a foul mood.

In the hall I notice Nikomedes and Kalchas preparing to leave for school.

"I'll bet Doros wins," Nikomedes says, shouldering his schoolbag.

"Not Aegisthes?" asks Kalchas with a raised eyebrow.

"Everyone at school says Doros will win."

I stop at the bottom of the stairs, remembering the conversation between the two men in the courtyard the night before. There was that name again. Doros.

"Do you know him?" I ask.

They look up, surprised to see me standing there.

"Of course," says Nikomedes. "Everybody does."

"I don't."

"That's because you're a girl."

He doesn't say it meanly, just matter-of-factly, as he might say the moon is round, but I can't help feeling the familiar sense of frustration for all that I have been deprived of because I was born female. The unfairness of it never ceases to rankle. It isn't fair that he gets to go to school and study mathematics and learn about philosophy and can go to the footraces and watch the equestrian processions, and I can't do any of these things because I'm a girl. Of course he can't go anywhere he wants and he has to put up with Kalchas dogging his steps wherever he goes, just as I have to put up with Zobia, but still it's a great deal more freedom than I have. I would trade places with him in a heartbeat.

"I heard he's rather homely," I say off-handedly. It gets just the reaction I hoped for.

"No way," says Nikomedes. "You must be thinking of someone else. Everyone says he looks like a god stepped down from Olympus. Isn't that right, Kalchas?"

But Kalchas is impatient to leave and won't play this game. "Enough. It's time to go. We don't want to keep your teachers waiting. You've been late once already this week, or have you forgotten?"

"That wasn't my fault," Nikomedes objects. "It was that gifts-for-the-bride-and-groom procession that made us late. We had to go at least two streets out of our way to get around it."

"And the time before that it was construction. Your teachers are losing patience with your excuses, and I don't blame them."

"Is it my fault they blocked off the street?" Nikomedes demands.

I can hear him arguing even after they are out the door. I pick up a pomegranate from a bowl on the side table, cut it open with a small knife and scoop some seeds into my mouth. Their tart sweetness fills my mouth. Sunlight spills into the courtyard as my cousin's words echo in my mind. *Like a god stepped down from Olympus.* Could this Doros really be as handsome as that? I imagine a young Adonis sprinting down the Panathenaic Way, graceful as a deer, muscles rippling.

"Rhea!"

I jump. Myrrine stands in the doorway leading to the courtyard, a frown on her face and a broom in her hand.

"Have you nothing to do this morning?" she asks rather crossly. "Aren't you needed upstairs?"

I'm in no rush to start sorting or spinning wool and I have every intention of finishing my pomegranate first, so I ignore the hint and follow her into the courtyard.

"Don't you ever wish that you could see the footraces?" I ask and take another bite of the sweet juicy seeds.

"No, I don't," she says, briskly sweeping the courtyard tiles. "It wouldn't be proper."

"I don't see why it isn't proper."

"The sight of men and boys racing by without a stitch of clothing isn't a proper sight for a woman of any age."

"I wouldn't be shocked," I insist. "I imagine they're quite beautiful. Like the statues in the Street of Statues."

She gives me a sideways glance. "Don't let your aunt hear you say that. She'll be taking your scrolls away for putting naughty ideas in your head."

She's probably right. My Aunt Damaris would welcome an excuse to confiscate my scrolls. But I'm not yet ready to abandon the topic and go upstairs to the loom room. I take another bite of juicy pomegranate while she sweeps energetically over the tiles. After I have swallowed, I try again.

"In Sparta the girls race too."

"The Spartans are little better than barbarians," she retorts.

"Atalanta raced. She wasn't a barbarian."

Myrrine shakes her head. "If you argue like this with your husband, he'll beat you for sure."

I sigh. She's probably right about this too. I remember Euphrastus with the flute girl in the garden and shudder. Is that the life I have to look forward to? A drunken husband who will try to corner me when he's in his cups and beat me when I speak my mind?

Before I can voice this thought, Zobia appears in the doorway. "Ah, here you are, Rhea. You're wanted upstairs. We need another pair of hands to help with sorting the wool."

I groan. Of course they do. With a last regretful glance up at the brightening sky, I leave Myrrine to her sweeping and reluctantly mount the stairs to join the women in the loom room. Everyone is expected to be useful, except of course old Xantippe, who seldom leaves her bed these days. Boring and tedious as it is, thread has to be made and cloth woven. As I have been told from the time I was old enough to pick up a ball of wool, clothes do not make themselves. If only they did!

In the hours that follow, my hands are busy sorting and combing wool, but my mind is busy thinking about Doros, the young athlete with the looks of a god. It seems so unfair that a girl has to spend her life cloistered behind the walls of her father's house, hardly ever meeting a boy who isn't a blood relative except for ones glimpsed during the

Panathenaic procession or at the plays — if she's fortunate enough to have parents who will take her — and they hardly count since she isn't allowed to speak to them. Then she is barely grown before she is married off to a man and cloistered behind *his* walls. Would it really hurt for me to see what I can never have — the young athlete Doros? In fact, if I did, what difference would it make? None that I can think of. It seems such a harmless thing to do, and the more I think about it, the more I realize I'd really like to see him, if only just once. The question is how. I can't exactly steal into his chamber by night with a candle like Psyche did with Eros, and anyway look how that turned out! Obviously I will need some help if I'm going to arrange a way to see him. And I can think of only one person who might be able to do that, my cousin Nikomedes. However, I'll have to ask him when Kalchas isn't around. It's bad enough to tell my young cousin what I want; I don't want Kalchas to know. He's sure to disapprove and might even tell my uncle. Then, like Psyche, I'll be in trouble for sure.

I get my opportunity to talk to Nikomedes after he comes home from school. When he steps into the courtyard as usual to see what's cooking, I'm there waiting to pounce.

"Did you go to the track today?" I ask brightly after he has asked what's for supper.

"Of course," he says. "I always go to practice after school."

I glance at Myrrine, who is hovering over the cooking pot with Merope, cooking the evening meal. They are talking and don't appear to be paying any attention to us.

"Did you see Aegisthes?" I ask, careful to keep my voice low so they won't overhear.

"Sure. He was there, practicing for the races."

"And Doros? Was he there too?"

"Yeah, him too. Why?"

I glance at the women again. Nikomedes follows my gaze.

"You know I'll have to marry soon?"

"Yeah."

"Once I'm married, I'll have to move to my husband's house and I'll have little freedom or chance to go out into the city."

"Sorry," he says, not meeting my eyes. "I'd help you if I could."

Now is my chance. I mustn't let it slip away. "I know there's nothing you can do about that, but there is something else you could do for me."

"What?" He sounds wary.

"You could help me see Doros."

He looks puzzled. "Why do you want to see him?"

I hesitate. But I know I'll have to explain, so I take a deep breath and let it out in a rush of words. "I'd just like to see with my own eyes if he's as handsome as everyone says."

To my relief he doesn't laugh. He considers this. "You know if I do this and Father hears about it, we could both get a beating."

Of course he's right. If we're found out, we'll probably be punished. I don't care for myself, but what right do I have to get Nikomedes in trouble? I start to turn away in disappointment.

"But if we're careful, he won't find out." He gives me a conspiratorial grin. I have suggested something sneaky that appeals to him.

"Then you'll help me?"

"Sure. Why not? What do you want me to do?"

I glance again at the two women hovering over the brazier. "I thought maybe you could invite him —"

He shakes his head. "It won't work."

"Why not?"

"It just won't."

"There must be some way —"

"Look, you just want to see him, right?"

"Yes."

"So all you have to do is be waiting nearby when school lets out. I'll be right behind him. That way you'll know who he is."

It's a simple plan. I feel a new respect for Nikomedes for having thought of it on the spur of the moment. I had no idea he was so clever.

"When?" I'm eager to put his plan into motion.

He shrugs. "Tomorrow?"

I can hardly believe it. With his help I have come up with a much better plan than Psyche did. No creeping about with a candle in the dark. I'll see Doros in the light of day. All I have to do is persuade Zobia to take me to the street that runs by Nikomedes' school in the late afternoon when classes are dismissing. Surely I can manage that.

CHAPTER 5

While I don't consider myself a devious person, since moving in with my aunt and uncle I've learned to be devious because it's the only way I can get out of the house. I know better than to ask my aunt for permission to leave. In the beginning I asked her and she always refused so I stopped asking. Even with Zobia I have to be devious. If I tell her why I want to go to the street that runs by Nikomedes' school, she'll never consent to go there. Instead I persuade her to walk with me to the cemetery outside the Dipylon Gate to visit my family's graves, which I know she won't refuse, and then because it's such a lovely autumn afternoon, I casually suggest we go look at the ash trees on the street near Nikomedes' school. Since it's only a little out of our way, she agrees.

That's how we come to be sitting on a bench facing the school but separated from it by a low stone wall when the boys begin to stream out at the end of the school day. They pour out in groups, older boys, younger boys, dressed in white tunics, long bare stork legs and sandals, talking animatedly and shoving each other. Their pedagogues trail behind more sedately in robes, talking to one another but keeping an eye on their young charges. I wish we were nearer, but Zobia insists we keep a respectable distance from the school. This is as close as I can persuade her to go, so I have to be content with it.

"You don't need to stare," she scolds as I scan the horde of boys. "Bad enough that we're here. I just hope nobody sees us." Her eyes dart about uneasily, but there are only a few passersby and they pay no heed to us.

"I'm not staring," I say. "I'm looking for Nikomedes."

"Since when are you so interested in your cousin?"

I ignore the question. I'm not going to let her spoil my enjoyment of the moment. I try to imagine what it must be like to go to school. "They look like they're having fun, don't they?" I feel a twinge of envy and wish once again that I had been born a boy so that I too could attend school.

"They look like a pack of young ruffians," Zobia sniffs, unimpressed.

I'm so used to the difference between our perspectives that I pay no attention to her comment. "I wonder what they learned today," I say wistfully, imagining lectures on mathematics, history, and philosophy.

"Little enough I'll wager," says Zobia, to whom they are only a pack of unruly boys.

I don't bother to argue. I'm too intent on catching a glimpse of Doros. There are so many boys I fear I'll miss him. Then, just as I begin to lose hope, I spot him, a fair-haired youth who walks with easy confidence and an athletic grace that sets him apart from the rest. How could I have thought I wouldn't know him when I saw him? The boys around him vie for his attention as if he were a hero of old, a Jason or a Perseus. He takes my breath away. I've never seen a boy so handsome. How could anyone look at him and not admire him? And there, a dozen paces behind, just as he promised, lopes Nikomedes, reed tall and gangly, with black-browed Kalchas close on his heels, deep in conversation with another pedagogue. I feel sorry for Nikomedes. He looks like a goose trailing a swan.

I touch Zobia's arm. "There! Do you see him?"

She squints nearsightedly at the stream of boys. "There are such a lot of them."

"Kalchas is just behind him. Surely you see Kalchas?"

She sighs and squints some more. "Yes, I think I do." Her voice does not carry much conviction.

I can't resist pointing out Doros too. "See that boy a few paces in front of Nikomedes? That's Doros, the young athlete everyone is talking about. They say he'll win the footraces."

"Well, they all look much the same to me."

I don't see how she can miss him, but her eyes are not as good as they used to be, as she frequently reminds me, and soon he's lost to sight, swallowed up by the horde of boys again. I look up at the blue afternoon sky. There is the smell of smoke in the air from the offerings the priests burn at the temples to appease the gods and lift the plague. A bird trills in the ash tree above us. I wish we could sit here a little longer, but Zobia is anxious for us to be on our way before the sun sinks lower in the sky.

* * *

And now, having seen Doros, I can't stop thinking about him. Seeing him has only whetted my appetite, not sated it. He's the handsomest boy I've ever set eyes on, the sort of youth the poets praise. I want to see him again, even if it's only another fleeting glimpse of him surrounded by his fellow students. But I know I won't be able to persuade Zobia to go to the school again so soon, especially not if she suspects why I want to go there, and a second time might well arouse her suspicions. What I need is a little divine intervention, so two days later I decide to climb the Acropolis again.

Perhaps I aimed too high when I appealed to Athena Parthenos on my previous visit. This time my destination will be the little temple of Athena Nike that stands on the edge of the Acropolis overlooking the Great Stair and the city below. She is far less intimidating than the monumental Great Goddess who towers over all in the Parthenon. Perhaps she will listen to my plea.

"Tell me again. Why are we doing this?" Zobia asks as we approach the little temple. She has grumbled all the way up the long stair, complaining about the number of steps and casting anxious glances at the grey overcast sky, worried that it's going to rain.

But I'm not about to explain. For two whole days I have thought of nothing but Doros. I have changed since I spotted him among the crowd of boys surging from the school. Now I understand what the poets are saying when they write of falling in love. Like Apollo, I have been struck by an arrow shot by Eros. One minute I feel elated thinking about Doros, and the next I'm plunged into despair, remembering that my aunt and uncle are arranging for me to marry the drunken lout Euphrastus. Surely the gods cannot be so cruel.

Taking a deep breath, I step with some trepidation into the portico of the little temple with its Ionic columns. What if the goddess refuses my offering of honey cake, I worry as I lay it on the altar under the eyes of a stern-faced priestess and peek into the inner sanctum at the small wooden statue of Nike, so much less imposing than the colossal ivory and gold statue of the Great Goddess in the Parthenon or the tall bronze warrior goddess with the gold-tipped spear that stands in the open air of the Acropolis.

The little temple is still under construction and part of it is roped off. We practically have it to ourselves. Zobia waits patiently while I do my obeisances. I invoke the goddess in a whisper too softly for anyone but her to hear: "Great Lady, hear my prayer . . ."

Like a true daughter of Athens, I ask her first for victory over Sparta, for she is the goddess of war and protector of our city. Then I ask for her to deliver us from the plague that has already claimed so many. These two civic issues having been addressed, I turn to my own personal concerns. I plead again to be spared from a marriage to Euphrastus. Last I ask that she grant me another glimpse of golden-haired Doros. *And this time let him notice me!* I draw out the minutes as long as I can, but at last I have no excuse to stay longer. As fate would have it, large drops of rain begin to fall as we turn to leave.

"I told you it was going to rain," mutters Zobia, clutching her mantle about her. "Now what shall we do?"

You would think we are under siege by the Spartans instead of merely at the mercy of a little rain.

"We'll just wait a bit for it to stop," I tell her, looking up at the pewter grey sky.

Since I'm not eager to return to my uncle's house, I don't really mind. It's far better to be out in the air and see the city spread out below us hemmed in by its wall, the rugged mountains beyond, and the sea in the distance. For a little while I can forget my problems and feel free.

We are standing near the edge of the portico when the wind suddenly blows the rain at us and cool wet drops fall on my bare arms soft as a caress.

"If we are late for dinner, your aunt will be upset," Zobia warns, clearly not savoring the moment as much as I am.

"We won't be late for dinner," I assure her. "We have plenty of time left."

As it continues to rain, a tall young man in a knee-length tunic runs toward us and ducks into the shelter of the portico. From his dark features as he stands dripping several feet away, I guess him to be a foreigner. This is not unusual since Athens has many foreigners.

Zobia casts a distrustful eye at him.

"You chose ill weather to pay a visit to the goddess," he remarks with no trace of an accent. He looks out at the rain and not at us, as if speaking to himself. He's older than I am, maybe eighteen or nineteen years old. He doesn't look particularly dangerous, nor does he look like one of the refugees that have fled their farms to seek sanctuary in the city while the Spartans ravage the countryside.

"It's only a little rain," I reply, just as studiously not looking at him.

At that moment a jagged flash of lightning streaks across the sky, followed by a loud clap of thunder. I hope I didn't jump.

"Zeus speaks," declares the young man. "Be careful what you say."

Zobia plucks at my arm, trying to pull me away. Respectable young women don't speak to strange men. But it's tiresome to always have to behave in a respectable manner. Besides, who's to know?

"I'm not afraid of a little rain," I say evenly.

The words are hardly out of my mouth when it begins to pour. Zobia clings to my arm, her face a mask of alarm.

"I hope you had better luck with the goddess than with Zeus," the young man says cheerfully, still not looking at me. "Please don't say you have no fear of being struck by lightning or I fear we may all perish when the next bolt strikes."

Jason used to dare me like that. 'Don't look at the old soothsayer in the marketplace. He'll make you break out in welts.' And of course I had to look at the old soothsayer just to show him I wasn't afraid.

"I'm not afraid of a little lightning." I lift my chin and stand a little straighter.

Sure enough, there is another flash, followed by an ear-splitting crack of thunder that makes Zobia jump.

"A girl who defies the gods," the young man says in mock amazement.

"I don't defy the gods," I retort.

"Enough," hisses Zobia. "Ignore him."

"No, I don't suppose you do." He glances now at me with a hint of amusement. He has bold dark eyes in a handsome chiseled face. "For if you did, you wouldn't be here asking the goddess for help. Let's see, what could bring a well brought up Athenian girl—as you appear to be—to beseech the goddess? You want your sweetheart to notice you. Or you want the goddess to bring him back to you after he's run off. Or perhaps he's out fighting Spartans."

"Why aren't *you* out fighting Spartans?" I snap back. "And I could ask you the same question. Why are you here to see the goddess? Are you looking for a little help from the gods when you compete with the discus or the javelin? Are you seeking help at the gaming table?"

"Wrong on both counts. I'm here to work on the friezes."

I look at him closer, curious now, my animosity gone. This completely changes things. I can't help being impressed. Sculptors, like poets, are beloved by the gods. And it explains why he isn't in the army. He has valuable skills needed to build and embellish the new monuments commissioned by Pericles. "You're a sculptor?"

"Not quite. I'm merely one of the many pairs of hands working under Kallikrates and Phidias."

Zobia lets out a small startled exclamation. She recognizes the names. As every Athenian knows, Kallikrates is one of the architects who designed the Parthenon and Phidias is the sculptor who made the great statues of Athena on the Acropolis. If the young man is a pair of hands working under them, he is most likely a slave. However, he doesn't seem like a slave. Most slaves would not have presumed to strike up a conversation with a freeborn Athenian girl of my station. If he's a slave, he's an impertinent one.

"Where are you from?" I ask before Zobia can stop me. "You're not Greek, are you?"

"I have no idea if I'm Greek or not, or where I'm from."

"It's time to go," Zobia declares, but I ignore her.

"You have no accent."

"That's because I've lived here since I was a child."

This intrigues me, although I try not to show it. "You have no memory of your homeland?"

"No, but many say I look Phrygian."

Since I'm not sure what a Phrygian looks like, I don't know if this is true.

"Would you show us what you're working on?" I ask, my curiosity to see his handiwork overcoming my desire to appear aloof and mature.

"You may look if you wish. It's a free world."

Not exactly an invitation, but it's enough for me.

He turns and enters the temple. I follow, Zobia close at my side, determined not to leave me alone with him for a second. The priestess tending the small fire by the altar watches us with hooded eyes. I feel my heart beat faster as we pass the small wooden statue of Athena Nike holding her helmet and a pomegranate branch. The helmet symbolizes war and the pomegranate branch symbolizes peace. I avert my eyes, hoping our presence does not offend the goddess, for I'll need all the help I can get if I'm to meet Doros or avoid an unwanted marriage.

The young man leads us to the other side of the temple

where a hammer and chisel lie beside some scaffolding. "That's what I'm working on," he says, pointing up at the frieze above our heads, where the image of warriors fighting is emerging from the marble. I can see their helmets and spears and even the folds of their tunics. "Greeks fighting the Persians," he explains, unable to keep a hint of pride from his voice.

"How do you make the figures so life-like?" I ask, awed by what I see. All of my reservations about him have vanished. He may be a slave, but he has a gift from the gods if he can sculpt like this.

"It's a craft like any other," he says simply. "I've been trained in it since I was old enough to hold a hammer and chisel."

"What do they call you?" I ask, looking at him with new eyes. He's handsome for a slave. In fact, had he not told us, I would not have known he is a slave. There is nothing about him — his hair, his tunic, his bearing — to mark him as other than a free man and citizen of Athens. Not that this is unusual. Visitors complain that it is not easy to distinguish slaves from free men when you encounter them in the streets of Athens.

"Maron. And what do they call you?"

"It's none of your business, young man," snaps Zobia, tugging at my arm.

I shake her off. To refuse to answer him would look arrogant, and I don't wish him to think I'm arrogant. He may be a slave, but he's also obviously intelligent and gifted as a sculptor. I lift my chin. "Rhea," I tell him.

"Like the mother-goddess?" He looks amused.

I feel myself color. "After my brother was born, the midwife told my mother she would have no more children. Then my mother prayed to the mother of the gods, and here I am. So they called me Rhea."

"Really," Zobia murmurs. "I'm sure this young man couldn't care less how you came by your name."

"How could I not care?" he protests. "It isn't every day I meet a goddess." He hurries on before Zobia can object. "I see you are a most devoted nurse. I'm sure the young lady's family has every confidence that you will watch out for her."

"I have watched over her since she was a babe," Zobia admits.

"And has she always been so headstrong?"

"That she has."

"Zobia!" I gasp. After all, he is a stranger and she has known me all my life. But she does not seem abashed.

"Well, it's time we left," she announces. "It's stopped raining."

I see with a twinge of disappointment that she is right. I would like to linger and talk a little more to Maron, but we have delayed long enough. It will take time to descend the Great Stair and make our way home. If we are late for dinner, my aunt and uncle will notice.

"A goddess indeed!" Zobia mutters, shaking her head as we walk away from the temple.

CHAPTER 6

Zobia scolds me all the way down the Great Stair, but I know she won't tell my aunt or uncle about our encounter with the sculptor-slave. We are locked together in a bond forged over my lifetime, and despite her grumbling, she will keep silent to protect me, so I hardly listen to her. My thoughts flit between Doros and Maron, the fair-haired athlete and the dark-eyed sculptor. I'm not quite sure why Maron has made such an impression on me. Maybe it's because I've never met anyone like him before. He isn't by any means a typical slave. He has about him a sense of self-confidence and independence that is, well, Greek. There's nothing subservient about him. He's obviously educated and intelligent. Handsome too, but in a different way than Doros, who is all sculpted muscle and grace and sweetness. It's a pity Maron is a slave, but there it is. We don't choose our destinies. Now if only I could find a way to meet Doros as easily as I met Maron.

All thoughts of both young men are swept out of my mind when we cross the threshold of my uncle's house. The household is in an uproar with the servants running about every which way.

"What now?" Zobia says beneath her breath.

I catch Myrrine's arm as she rushes toward the kitchen with an empty krater and an anxious expression on her face. "What's happened?" I ask her.

"Damaris's sister is ill and she's gone to nurse her."

My stomach drops. "Is it the plague?" Of course that's the first thing I think of since so many have already died of it. I dread hearing that anyone has fallen sick.

"We don't know."

I hear Zobia moan softly beside me.

"They don't know for sure," I tell her. "Maybe it's just a fever that will soon pass." I chatter like that all the way upstairs, trying to reassure her. Maybe it's really myself I'm trying to reassure. The memory of losing my family to the plague is still fresh.

Later, after eating supper in the courtyard with the other women, I retreat to my room intending to curl up with a scroll and read by lamplight, but as I'm lifting a scroll from my chest, Myrrine appears in the doorway.

"Your uncle wants to see you," she says, looking worried.

"What does he want?" I ask warily.

"I don't know, but you'd best not keep him waiting."

I sigh and drop the scroll back into my chest, then hurry downstairs. I wonder if he's heard about my outing to the Acropolis. Is he going to punish me for leaving the house without permission?

I find him in his study working on his accounts and wait respectfully by the door for permission to enter.

"What is it?" he asks impatiently when he finally notices me standing there.

"Myrrine said you wanted to see me."

His brow knits. "So I did. Well, don't just stand there like a common slave girl. Come in."

I take a deep breath and step into the room. It's like plucking up courage to enter the den of a mountain lion.

"I believe your aunt told you about this marriage prospect that has arisen?" His eyes are on the papyri spread out on a table in front of him. I can't tell what he's thinking. There's no smile to put me at ease, just the usual scowl.

At least it's not about my visit to the Acropolis. For that I heave a sigh of relief. I try to choose my words carefully so I won't seem ungrateful. "She has, and I appreciate what you're trying to do for me and how you've taken me in, but—"

He stops me with a raised hand. "I only did a brother's duty."

"I'm very grateful," I assure him, trying to be tactful, "but I would like to wait a little longer. It's only been a month since—" I was going to say a month since my father died but again he interrupts me.

"All the more reason to do it. It'll help take your mind off your loss."

I feel panic rising within me and try to quell it. I must make him understand that I'm not ready to be a wife. "If I had just another year . . ."

"Enough!" The anger in his voice stops me cold. He's glaring at me. I drop my eyes.

I know I should hold my tongue, yet how can I? My future is at stake and I'm not permitted to argue on my own behalf? I'm an orphan now and who will stand up for me if I can't stand up for myself? My uncle, who is supposed to protect me, is planning to sacrifice me for the sake of a debt. The injustice of it is hard to bear. I look at the floor and try to control my turbulent emotions. He is my uncle and I'm not supposed to argue with him.

"It was in fact regarding your marriage that I wanted to speak to you," he continues, the anger gone now or at least restrained. "I wanted to let you know that a date has been set. You'll be wed at the next full moon."

The next full moon is only a month away. I had hoped for more time. I feel as if the world is closing in on me.

"The times are uncertain," he says. "Best to get this taken care of quickly."

"Couldn't it wait a little longer?" I plead. "I could work on my linens." Linens are part of the dowry a bride is expected to bring to her marriage. I know I'm grasping at straws. What do I care for linens? But he doesn't know that, and so perhaps it will give him pause.

He frowns. "A girl your age should already have sewed her linens. Your mother should have seen to this."

My anger flares at this implied criticism of my mother, but I choke it back. I won't marry Euphrastus if I can help it. I'll run away. I'll kill myself if I have to. Death is preferable to such a marriage. But even as these defiant thoughts race through my mind, I know in the end I will have to obey my uncle. It's a bitter fate, every bit as awful as being sacrificed like poor Iphigenia burned alive on a beach in Aulis to appease the goddess Artemis before her father sailed for Troy. How will I bear it?

My heart is heavy as I climb the stairs. Zobia is in the loom room sorting wool with Myrrine and Merope. I throw myself down beside her and lay my head in her lap, just as I used to when I was a child.

"Oh, Zobia, what am I to do?" I moan. "My uncle says the marriage will take place at the next full moon."

"There, there," she says, patting my head. "Crying will do no good. Perhaps marriage won't be as bad as you think."

I rub a hand across my eyes. "That's easy for you to say. You don't have to marry that awful man."

"You'll have to make the best of it," Myrrine says matter-of-factly, her fingers moving with practiced ease among the strands of wool. "It's a woman's lot."

"That it is," chimes in Merope, who has a scar over one eyebrow from a beating given her by a previous owner. "Better get used to it."

But I don't want to get used to it. I don't see why my destiny has to be yoked to a man like Euphrastus. Why can't my uncle find someone else for me to marry? Why can't Athena help me out?

Later, long after the house has fallen still, I lie awake trying to think of a way out of my dilemma. Perhaps because I'm depressed, I can think of nothing short of falling ill of the plague and dying, which of course reminds me of my family and makes me feel even more miserable. In the end I cry myself to sleep and dream of going home and finding them alive and well. If only it were real and not just a dream.

CHAPTER 7

In the morning I wake up to hard reality again. My family is gone and my aunt and uncle are preparing to marry me off to a man I despise. I wish that I could run home and find my family alive and well as they were in my dream, but I know they won't be there. They are in the underworld now, or at least their shades are. Their mortal remains are in the cemetery outside the Dipylon Gate, and if I want to talk to them, that is where I must go. Of course Zobia would go with me if I ask her, but I want to be alone and it's not far from my uncle's house so I wait until she lies down for an afternoon nap to steal away.

Once outside I walk quickly with my head down and my mantle covering my head. Maybe it was a mistake not to bring Zobia along. Being alone makes me feel vulnerable, though of course, as my aunt pointed out, what could an old woman do if we found ourselves in a dangerous situation? But my fears prove unfounded. The few men I encounter barely glance at me. I pass through the heavy wooden doors of the Dipylon Gate without incident and arrive safely at the cemetery. Once there I have the place to myself. There is no one around except for some gravediggers. It's a warm day and the afternoon sun reflects off the stele, monuments, columns, and statues as I weave among them.

I know my way by heart to the graves of my family. When I reach them, I sit on the low stone wall nearby and let my mantle fall back, leaving my head bare. I close my eyes and feel the warm sun on my face as I think about my family and how much I miss them. It seems like only yesterday that I walked through the streets by torchlight with their funeral processions. I remember the wailing and the pouring of libations of wine and olive oil over their graves and my own inconsolable grief. And yet I have survived. It hardly seems possible that they are gone. I would give anything to have them back again. How I miss them! I feel so alone. I have no one to turn to for advice, no one to look out for me. If only my mother were here to counsel me! Or Jason. Yes, my brother Jason would have known what to do about this unwanted marriage my aunt and uncle are arranging for me. From the time I took my first steps, I looked up to him, and he looked out for me. Now how empty the world seems without him!

My reverie is interrupted by the sound of approaching footsteps. I look down, hoping the intruder will respect my grief and pass by, but instead he stops a few feet behind me. Annoyed, I turn to see who's there. To my surprise it's Maron, the sculptor-slave I met at the temple of Athena Nike yesterday.

"What are you doing here?" I ask.

"I'm working on a portrait on a stele over there." He points toward the gravediggers. "I might ask you the same question. Why are you here, and where's your nurse?" He glances about as if Zobia might be hiding behind a stele.

"I left her at home."

"I'm surprised she agreed to that."

"I didn't give her a choice." No need to mention that she was sleeping.

"You aren't afraid to walk alone in the streets?" he asks, quirking an eyebrow. Again I notice his dark intelligent eyes and his handsome chiseled face. Zobia would be upset if she knew I was sitting here unchaperoned talking to him.

I lift my chin. "My uncle's house isn't far from here."

"I might have been a thief," he suggests.

"But you aren't. Or at least I don't think you are."

He ignores this. "A relative?" he asks, nodding at the stele.

"My mother and father. And next to them, my brother."

He looks appropriately somber. "I'm sorry. Was it the plague?"

I nod, my throat suddenly tight.

"So now you live with your uncle?"

"My aunt and uncle."

"And are they good to you?"

"Yes, but I miss my family."

"Of course you do."

Tears spring to my eyes at his kind words and I turn my head so he won't see them. "I just can't believe they're gone." I dab the corner of my eye with my mantle.

"I'm sorry," he says again.

And now the words come rushing out as if I've been keeping them dammed up inside. "My brother was so strong, so alive. Everyone said he would be a great warrior. He was supposed to sail with a naval expedition in another month. If he had, maybe he wouldn't have caught the plague."

"Or maybe he would have died at sea or on a battlefield."

I stare at him for a minute, pulled up short. "Maybe so, but I think he would have preferred that."

"He would still have been dead."

"But he would have had fame and honor."

"Like Achilles."

I nod. "Like Achilles." The most famous Greek hero of all.

He looks thoughtfully at the gravediggers in the distance. "Do you know what Achilles said when Odysseus met him in the underworld?"

I shake my head. I'm not sure I care what Achilles said. He tells me anyway.

"Better to be the lowliest farmer in life than a hero in the world of the dead."

Maybe that's true, but it sounds vaguely treasonous when every able-bodied young Greek yearns to be a hero. It also surprises me that a slave would know Homer. But then clearly Maron is no ordinary slave.

"You don't know anything about it," I say.

"Maybe not. I confess I have lost no one to the plague. But then I have no one to lose."

I'm not sure if I pity him or envy him. In any case he will be spared the pain of losing a loved one. "It's so unfair. It ought to have been me who died."

He looks at me hard. "Don't ever say that. Your brother would have wanted you to be strong."

Maybe he's right, but it doesn't help. "It's so hard to go on alone without them."

"You have your aunt and uncle."

I grimace. "They're making plans to marry me off." I can't keep the bitterness out of my voice.

"Well, then you won't be alone."

I shake my head. "You don't understand. I don't want to get married. Especially not to the man they've chosen."

His eyes slide again to the gravediggers on the far side of the cemetery. "And what's so bad about the man they've chosen?"

I take a deep breath. "He's old and ugly and he looks like a murderer. In fact, I wouldn't be surprised if he is."

"That's rather harsh. Surely your aunt and uncle wouldn't wed you to anyone disreputable. They have their family honor to think of."

Was there a hint of sarcasm in his voice? His face gives me no clue. "It seems my uncle owes him money," I explain. "A gambling debt."

"And your inheritance will repay that debt?"

"Apparently." The injustice of it rises up before me again, like a serpent rearing its head. "I don't see how the gods can be so cruel."

"I doubt the gods have anything to do with it."

"I prayed to Athena Parthenos."

"And Athena Nike," he reminds me.

At mention of Athena Nike, I remember why I went to her temple. It wasn't just about the marriage to Euphrastus. I went there to pray for Doros to notice me. I feel the blood rush to my face.

"Does this man you're to marry have a name?" he asks.

"Euphrastus, son of Linus," I answer, relieved that he didn't notice my confusion. "Do you know him?"

He shakes his head. "No. But perhaps he's not so bad. You can't always judge a man by his looks."

And sometimes you can, I think to myself, remembering how the moonlight fell on that cruel face with its ugly scar.

"You don't understand," I tell him again. "It's different for you. You're a man. Nobody will force you to marry someone against your will."

"I'm a man," he agrees, "but I'm also a slave. Do you think that's so wonderful? In a city that extols freedom? Does no one see the irony in that?"

"You may not always be a slave," I point out since sometimes slaves are given their freedom or save up money and buy their freedom. "And you hardly seem like a typical slave. You're educated. You move about the city freely."

"But I must also do what I'm told. My master rents me out like a horse or a donkey."

I have to admit that sounds bad, but I still don't think his situation is worse than mine. I try again to explain. "If you are given your freedom, you can go anywhere you want. You can even leave Athens."

"I'd like that," he says.

This shocks me. It's practically heresy to say you would

like to leave Athens, which as everyone knows is the most civilized city in the world. We are fortunate to be Athenians. Not that there aren't places elsewhere I would like to visit. But to choose to leave? I find this difficult to comprehend.

"Where would you go?" I ask, curious.

"I don't know. Maybe Phrygia. Perhaps I could find out if that's where I'm from. Or Olympia, to see the great statue of Zeus. There are all sorts of places I'd like to see. What about you? If you could go anywhere, where would you go?"

I hesitate. "I don't know. I never really thought about it."

"There must be someplace you'd like to go."

I think of Sappho and her wonderful poems. "The island of Lesbos."

"What's at Lesbos?"

"That's where Sappho was born."

He raises an eyebrow. "Does that mean you can read?"

"My father taught me," I answer with pride.

"And I thought you were just another empty-headed, love-struck Athenian girl when I saw you at the temple of Athena Nike."

He has struck so near the truth that I feel the blood rush to my cheeks again. This time he notices.

"But that's it, isn't it?" he says, snapping his fingers. "That's why you were there. You've met someone and you've fallen in love. It's not just this husband your aunt and uncle have picked out that made you turn to Athena for help. There's someone else. I should have guessed."

I don't know what to say. I feel embarrassed and avoid his eyes.

"Do your aunt and uncle know?"

I shake my head. "No. They would never understand. What do you think I should do?"

He considers for a minute. "Do you really want to know what I think?"

I nod.

"Well, if I were you, I'd move heaven and earth to follow my heart and to hell with what other people wanted for me."

The boldness of his words both shock and thrill me. He has so much confidence. I doubt I could ever be that confident. I can't just refuse to marry the man my aunt and uncle have chosen. It would be disrespectful. I wonder if Maron has ever faced such a quandary.

"Have you ever been in love?" I ask on impulse. At once I realize I should not have asked such a personal question to a man I hardly know, but fortunately Maron doesn't seem to think I have overstepped the bounds of propriety.

"No, I don't suppose I have. Not unless you count a dancer I met in the Ceramicus one night when I was drunk, and I don't really remember that so clearly. But I think I told her I loved her. At the time I meant it too."

I'm fairly certain he shouldn't be talking to me about dancers in the Ceramicus. And I'm disappointed he has not taken my question seriously.

"I should go back," I announce abruptly, rising. "They'll wonder what happened to me."

"Can't you stay a few more minutes?"

"I've stayed long enough."

He sighs. "Then I'll walk with you."

I hesitate. How will I explain if someone from my uncle's household or a neighbor sees me walking with him and tells my uncle? "That isn't necessary," I assure him.

But Maron seems oblivious to my concerns. "Well, if you won't let me walk with you, I'll follow you. Just to make sure you get back safely."

"I'm sure I'll be perfectly safe."

I start walking and true to his word he follows a few paces behind. This seems even more conspicuous than walking side by side, so I wait for him to catch up, resigned to the gossip that may result.

"Shouldn't you be working?" I suggest, glancing back toward the cemetery. But he doesn't take my hint.

"Don't worry. Soon enough I'll be back to my labors."

We have just passed through the Dipylon Gate when I see an old man huddled against a wall, probably a beggar, maybe a refugee from the countryside. He watches us approach and stretches out a skinny hand for alms. "In the name of the gods," he croaks.

Maron lays a hand on my arm. "Don't touch him!"

I notice the old man's rheumy eyes, blotched skin, and the beads of perspiration on his brow. Frightened, I look away and we walk a little faster.

"Do you think he has the plague?" I ask nervously.

"Best not to take chances," Maron answers.

I stop and face him. He is at least a head taller than I am. His dark eyes stare back at me. "We should part here," I tell him firmly. "I live only a few doors down."

He nods, and this time when I move forward, he doesn't follow, but I feel his eyes watching me as I continue up the street.

CHAPTER 8

As soon as I step into the house, I know something is wrong. My aunt and uncle are arguing with raised voices in his study. Myrrine rushes by with a heap of linens in her arms and sees me hovering by the door.

"Where have you been?" she demands. Before I can answer, she gives a curt nod toward the stairs. "Go up to Zobia. She's half out of her mind with worry. What were you thinking going out alone? Lucky for you your aunt and uncle are too busy to notice."

"What's happening?" I ask. "Why are they arguing?"

"Never mind. This has nothing to do with you." She shoos me toward the stairs.

I don't wait to be told a second time. Grateful not to be in trouble, I hurry up to the loom room, where I find Zobia sorting strands of wool with Merope while tears trickle down her creviced cheeks. When she sees me, she lets out a cry of relief and drops the wool into a basket by her feet.

I feel a pang of guilt as she hugs me. "Thank the gods," she says. Then just as abruptly she pushes me away. "You bad girl. Where have you been? I thought you'd been snatched by a slave trader or worse."

"I just went to the cemetery." I don't mention running into Maron. That would only upset her more. "What's happening downstairs?"

"Your aunt came home an hour ago. She says she's going back to her sister again, but your uncle forbids it."

"Why?"

"Her sister . . . has the plague." Zobia whispers as if it might be bad luck to say it aloud. Her eyes brim with tears. So it's not for me she has been weeping but for Damaris.

"Won't she catch it?" I ask uneasily, remembering how my parents sent me away when the plague struck our house.

Zobia closes her eyes and shakes her head. Merope gives me a hard look.

I have never known my aunt to defy my uncle before, and I can hardly believe she is doing so now. I understand my uncle's concern. She must know that she's risking her own life by nursing her sister. I remember only too well how helpless I felt as one by one my family died.

"Will he let her go?"

Zobia bends down to retrieve her wool from the basket and sighs. "How can he stop her?"

We soon find out the answer. He can't. She may defer to him in most things, but in this she's like one of those iron-willed women in a tragedy by Sophocles or Euripides. Nothing anyone can say will sway her. Her mind is made up.

And so in the middle of the afternoon she walks out of the house, taking Merope with her.

You would think that my aunt's departure would totally disrupt the household, but instead routine continues as usual. There is still thread to be spun, cloth to be woven, floors to be swept, and meals to be prepared. The day after she leaves I'm in the loom room, helping with the spinning, my hands busy, my mind wandering. My thoughts revolve around Doros. I imagine a dozen different ways to see him again. I imagine meeting him by accident in the marketplace or on the street, but the likelihood of either of these happening is small since I'm not supposed to leave the house. Clearly I must figure out a way to go out if I'm to see him. In the end I decide to turn to Nikomedes again for help.

The hours pass slowly as I wait for him to return from school. I keep glancing at the sunlight slanting into the loom room through the narrow windows and making white bars of light on the floor. It seems as if the afternoon will never end. I'll die of boredom. After what seems like an eternity, I hear the door downstairs slam. At last Nikomedes and Kalchas are home. Of course I can't rush down right away — it would attract too much notice — so I count to one hundred, then stretch.

"My back is aching from holding the distaff so long," I announce. "I think I need a break."

Zobia throws a suspicious glance at me, but Lede, who is helping sort and card wool now that Merope is gone, doesn't even look up. She's a plain woman, older than Myrrine, and walks with a bit of a limp as a result of an accident she had while young.

Before they can object, I'm out the door, racing barefoot down the stairs and out through the open doorway into the courtyard, where Nikomedes has just squatted down to play a game of pebbles.

"I used to play that with Jason," I say, squatting beside him on the tiles.

"You want to play?"

"Sure."

He hands me a few grey pebbles. "Once he gave me an old silver coin with the head of Zeus on it."

That sounds like Jason all right. He never hoarded treasures. He always gave them away. "I miss him," I say.

"What do you suppose it's like when you die?" Nikomedes tosses his head to get his hair out of his eyes. "Do you suppose it's like in the stories — you know, crossing the river Styx and being trapped in Hades? I'd like to see the three-headed dog, but I don't think I'd care for the rest of it."

"Me neither," I say with a grimace, "though I'd like to see my mother and father and Jason again. Of course it wouldn't be the same . . ."

"No, they would be shades."

I watch as he aims one pebble at another. They make a little click as he hits his target. I know if I'm going to ask him to help me, I have no time to lose. Kalchas could appear at any moment and call him away.

"Would you help me see Doros again?" I ask in a low voice so Myrrine, who is tending the cooking pot, won't hear. I glance at her. She is absorbed in her work and isn't paying any attention to us.

"Why do you want to see him?" Nikomedes aims another pebble and this time misses.

"I have my reasons."

He cocks his head to one side and looks at me through the unruly lock of hair. "Are you in love with him?"

I feel my face go hot. "Of course not. I don't even know him. How could I be in love with him?"

He shrugs. "Then why do you want to see him?"

I aim one of my pebbles at his and miss. Asking him for help is harder than I expected. "I just do. And this time, I want to talk to him."

"How are you going to do that?" Nikomedes asks. "He's always surrounded by people."

"There must be a way."

He shoots another pebble. "Sometimes he goes to the agora after school."

Just then Kalchas' voice booms out. "Nikomedes!"

We both jump.

He stands in the doorway scowling at us. "Your father wants to talk to you. *Now.*"

Scooping up his pebbles with one sweep of his hand, Nikomedes leaps to his feet.

I wonder if Kalchas overheard us. I don't think he did, but when I get up to follow Nikomedes into the house, he blocks my way.

"Why do you want to see Doros?" he demands.

I feel my face redden but stand a little straighter, determined not to be intimidated. "I want to ask him something."

"What?"

I glare at him. I'm not about to tell him why I want to see Doros.

"Do you know him?"

"No."

"Then you have no business seeking him out."

I don't argue. Kalchas couldn't possibly understand. There's no point in trying to explain to him. I wonder if he'll tell my uncle. I hope not.

"Look, I know you're unhappy about your coming marriage," he says more gently. "But there's nothing you can do about it. Accept it. The gods don't always give us what we want."

Does he think I don't know that? But couldn't they give us what we want once in a while?

"So I'm supposed to just marry Euphrastus?" I say, unable to hold my anger in check. "That's it? I might as well lie down and die."

"I'm saying, forget about Doros."

We have a staring match then, neither willing to be the first to look away. He has dark absolutely impenetrable eyes. I wonder how many things he has had to forget to endure his life in bondage. Did he leave a wife behind? Children? Has he resigned himself to being a slave for the rest of his life? Well, maybe he has resigned himself to his fate, but I haven't resigned myself to mine. Life may be closing in on me, but I'm not ready to give up.

CHAPTER 9

There's just one problem with my plan to go to the agora this afternoon on the chance of seeing Doros again. Women seldom go to the agora, at least not respectable women. Of course female slaves and women of the lowest ranks work at some of the stalls, but mostly the agora is the domain of men. They sell their goods and services there and do the shopping for their households or send male slaves to do it for them. And since the war with Sparta and the influx of people from the countryside, it's crowded with beggars and laborers looking for work. Damaris would never allow me to go there, but now that she's not here, it's only Zobia I need to persuade.

Fortunately I hit upon a brilliant reason for why we should go to the agora. I tell her I need a new pair of sandals.

"Why not have a sandal maker come here?" she suggests when I have complained for a good half hour about how my sandals are wearing out. "That's what your Aunt Damaris would do."

We are sitting in the loom room, just the two of us since Myrrine is still working downstairs and Lede is attending to old Xantippe.

"Please can't we go to the agora?" I plead. "It would do me good to get out in the fresh air, and it would be so much faster than having a sandal maker come here."

"You were just out in the fresh air yesterday," she reminds me.

"You could compare prices," I say, knowing this will appeal to her thrifty nature.

She hesitates, clearly tempted. "It isn't seemly for a young woman to go to the agora."

"I'll wear my mantle," I promise. "I'll cover my head."

She sighs. "I doubt your aunt would approve."

I give her a quick hug, knowing I have won the argument. Lycurgus left the house immediately after breakfast to attend an Assembly at the Pnyx, but it's unlikely he would have given us permission to go to the agora. We both know this.

Once I have persuaded her, I need to delay our outing until late afternoon so it will coincide with the end of the school day. That's when Nikomedes said Doros would be there. Timing is everything and I feel elated when all goes according to my plan and we arrive at the agora exactly when we should. However, there is no sign of Doros. I'm disappointed, but there's so much else to look at that I don't fret. As usual, the marketplace is noisy and full of life. I try to take it all in—fruit stalls, fishmongers, pottery for sale, wool and flax and linen, silver jewelry, olive oil, spices, and the citizens, slaves, and foreigners who have come to buy or sell their wares or just browse and talk.

I could stand here forever just watching people and not get bored, but Zobia, ever practical, heads straight for the leather stalls. After looking them over with a skeptical eye, she begins to haggle with a lean sunburnt leather-worker with a beard and one blind eye. After they agree on a price, a piece of leather is spread on the ground and I'm instructed to step on it while a tow-headed slave boy outlines my feet with a piece of chalk. As he works, I keep an eye on the marketplace, watching for Doros. The boy has just finished my right foot when I notice a young woman in a sea-green ankle-length tunic and matching mantle walking toward us. She's accompanied by a more plainly dressed female slave. As she approaches the leather stall, her voice seems familiar, as does the lithe grace with which she moves. She is shorter in stature than me with blue eyes, pale translucent skin, and a dimpled smile.

"I know you," I say in surprise as she shakes her pretty head free of her mantle. "You're the flute girl."

She tilts her head, studying me. A look of recognition lights her face. "Oh, you're the young lady on the balcony the other night. The one who's to marry the big man with the scar." She runs a forefinger down her cheek, indicating the scar, then grimaces. "I don't envy you."

"I want to thank you for what you did," I tell her. "Zobia, do you have an obol I can give her?"

"Oh, forget it," says the girl. "It was nothing."

Zobia, grumbling, fishes an obol out of her belt and hands it to me. I hold it out to the girl, who hesitates only a second, then takes it with a shrug and drops it into a small purse she carries tied to her wrist.

"Did you know he's been married before?" she asks.

I stare at her. "No, I didn't. What happened to his wife?"

"She died in childbirth."

"Poor woman," Zobia mutters and spits to ward off evil. She is looking over the flute girl as if trying to decide if she is dangerous or not.

"They had a baby girl," the flute girl explains. "People say he had a servant take her up on a mountain and leave her to die."

"Hestia, have mercy," says Zobia, invoking the goddess of the hearth.

At this moment a noisy crowd of boys invade the agora. We turn our heads to watch. And there he is, his golden head contrasting with the dark locks of his friends, a young god surrounded by mere mortals. The boys' pedagogues saunter several paces behind, their eyes sweeping the marketplace, keeping an eye out for trouble. Suddenly my plan to speak to Doros seems foolish. What was I thinking? How could I possibly walk up to him with all eyes in the agora on me?

"He's a handsome fellow," the flute girl remarks.

I hastily look away, hoping I wasn't staring. A glance at Zobia reassures me that she hasn't noticed. She has turned back to the leather-worker and is paying no attention to us or the boys.

"He'll break some poor girl's heart with those golden curls and those shoulders," the flute girl says, her eyes still fixed on Doros.

"They say he's going to win the footrace at the festival," I tell her, trying to sound nonchalant.

"If he's as good a runner as he is handsome, he's sure to win. Don't you think so, Metis?"

Her chaperone says nothing, just watches us with big dark wary eyes.

"Her Greek is only so-so," Chloe confides in an aside. "I'm trying to help her improve, but she's either very dull or not much interested in learning."

I look down at my feet. The boy has finished outlining my left foot. I step out of the markings and back into my sandals.

"I don't even know your name," I murmur to the girl while Zobia arranges to have the new sandals delivered to our house.

The flute girl smiles. She has pretty even teeth and again I notice the dimple. "Chloe. I live in the Ceramicus in the street just beyond the Street of Potters."

The boy has now spread another piece of leather on the ground and is waiting patiently for her to slip off her sandals and step on it.

"Will I see you again?" I ask, knowing that in another moment Zobia will want to leave.

She shrugs. "Who knows? Perhaps I'll play my flute at your wedding."

"I don't think I'll feel like dancing."

"Then I'll play a sad song, and all your guests will weep."

"Weep?" Zobia turns toward us. She has been listening after all. "At a wedding? What nonsense. Now come along, Rhea. We're done here."

I would like to stay and talk to the flute girl longer, but

Zobia is hobbling away. The girl is closely watching the tow-headed slave boy outline her foot. She tells him to leave a little extra space for her toes. With a last regretful glance back, I dart after Zobia.

As we make our way out of the agora, I notice the boys and their pedagogues have stopped at a fruit stall and are good-naturedly haggling for figs. Doros is at the heart of the group. I wonder if I'll ever get to speak to him, if there will ever be a time when he isn't surrounded by friends and chaperoned by a pedagogue. He might as well be a god on Olympus. I'd have just about as much chance of getting his attention.

"Why the long face?" Zobia asks as we turn into the Street of Statues. "You have sighed half a dozen times since we left the agora. I thought going there would make you happy."

I can't tell her about Doros. She'll just scold me. After all, I'm supposed to marry Euphrastus. Zobia may be sympathetic, but she can't get me out of the marriage that my aunt and uncle have arranged. And now I know one more awful fact about my future husband.

"Did you hear what she said about Euphrastus?" I ask her. "That he's been married before?"

"That's not a crime," Zobia says.

"And he put his baby daughter out on a mountain to die."

"As many others have done."

I stop and look at her. "What if I give birth to a daughter? Will he do the same to her?"

She sighs and puts her arm around me. "I don't know,

Little One. I just don't know. You must be brave. It's in the hands of the gods."

CHAPTER 10

I am awakened in the night by wailing—a dreadful lonely otherworldly sound that sends chills down my spine. In the moonlight I can see Zobia lying on her bed. Rising, I go to her and touch her arm.

"Do you hear it?" I whisper.

Another wail breaks the silence of the night.

"The gods preserve us." Zobia wraps her arms around me and pulls me close as if she will protect me from whatever horror lurks without.

"What is it?"

When she doesn't answer, I shiver and huddle closer. Downstairs someone pounds on the street door.

"Wait here." Zobia releases me and reaches for her belt, which she quickly ties around the waist of her tunic.

I don't want to be left alone in the dark with that awful sound. I grab my belt too, tying it with trembling fingers as I hurry after her into the hall. Myrrine and Lede are there, their hair down, shawls clutched about them. Even Lycurgus's old mother, Xantippe, is there, tottering unsteadily, eyes wide with fear. They hover at the top of the stairs, conferring in low voices. Zobia makes her way through them and starts down, one hand on the railing to steady her.

I can hear men's voices below — Lycurgus and Kalchas — then a woman's voice, rapid and indistinct.

"It's a servant from next door," says Myrrine. "I recognize her voice."

We whisper nervously and move closer together, like sheep huddling during a storm. I take Myrrine's hand and wonder if she's frightened too.

Soon Zobia returns, out of breath from climbing the stairs. "Our neighbor has fallen ill," she tells us. "Kalchas has gone to fetch a physician. The Master says we're to go back to bed. There's nothing more to be done tonight."

Nervously we return to our rooms.

"Do you think it's the plague?" I ask her when we are alone again.

"Who knows? Maybe it was something he ate or an attack of gout. Try to go back to sleep."

I suspect like me she thinks it's the plague and is trying to keep me from worrying. The wailing continues sporadically for a long time, but eventually I fall asleep.

When I wake in the morning, it has stopped. Nervously I splash water on my face and tie back my hair. When I go downstairs, everyone looks tired and worried and no one seems inclined to talk. We eat in silence, each wrapped in our own thoughts.

Later in the loom room with Zobia and Lede, I can't stop thinking about the wails I heard in the night. Damaris's loom stands abandoned, the cloth she was weaving half finished. No one wants to touch it. It would seem like a bad omen, as if we don't expect her to return. Mechanically we go about our work of sorting, combing, and spinning. I feel oppressed by the futility of it. Finally I can bear it no longer. I fling my wool in the basket and head for the door.

"Rhea!" Zobia calls after me. "Where are you going?"

I don't stop to answer. Instead I walk faster. I hurtle down the stairs, knowing that I must get out of the house or I'll suffocate. I stop only long enough to slip my sandals on and then I fling the door open and stand blinking in the bright light of day, gulping in the air, my head bare under the blue sky. How can the world look so beautiful when so much is wrong? I start running, although my ankle-length tunic hampers me. I don't know where I'm going. Does it matter? I avert my eyes from the house next door as if the mere sight of it could cause contagion. Is there nowhere in the city free from the threat of plague? Where can I go? Not the agora. It will be crowded and I don't feel like being surrounded by people. The narrow winding streets beyond the Street of Statues then.

I run until I'm out of breath and my side hurts. Looking about me, I find I'm in the Ceramicus, where tradesmen live and work, a rougher part of the city than where my aunt and uncle live. It occurs to me that I must be close to the street where Chloe, the flute girl, lives. I see a woman in a bright blue mantle walking ahead of me and decide to ask her for directions.

"Can you tell me where the Street of Potters is?" I ask, catching up to her.

When she turns to look at me, I see she is a young woman with a beautiful face and rings on her fingers. She must be a hetaira or she wouldn't be in the street alone. She would have a slave with her.

She looks at me with kind eyes. "Go right at the next corner. You'll find yourself in the Street of Potters."

I thank her. She smiles and then turns aside and slips into a house, leaving me alone again.

Once I find the Street of Potters, I soon find the next street, where Chloe said she lives. However, which sun-bleached house on the narrow crowded street is hers? I can't just knock on doors and ask for her. It wouldn't be proper. So I wander along the street hemmed in by houses on both sides, feeling more and more discouraged. I'm about to give up and turn back when I hear a flute. It must be her! My spirit soars and I shout her name. The flute stops abruptly. A moment later a nearby door is flung open, and Chloe stands there in the doorway, wildly beckoning to me.

As I approach, she puts a warning finger to her lips and without a word pulls me inside. We tiptoe up a stairway. At the top we duck into the first room we come to. Then she hugs me like a long-lost sister. When she releases me, I see we're not alone. A younger girl dressed in a short tunic stands nearby watching us, her auburn hair falling in ringlets on either side of her pretty face.

"This is Nessa," Chloe says by way of introduction. "She can stand on her head. Show her, Nessa."

The younger girl stoops, plants her delicate hands on the

floor, and in slow motion does a headstand, then gracefully arching her back, comes down, legs sliding apart until she sits before us in the splits position as if it were the most natural thing in the world. I stare at her in astonishment. She's a tumbler, no doubt part of the same troupe of entertainers as Chloe.

"What do you do?" Nessa asks, regarding me gravely. She can't be more than eight or nine.

"She's freeborn," Chloe says with a toss of her head. "She doesn't have to do anything."

"I can read," I say, which is the only accomplishment that I can think of for the moment. From the blank expression on Nessa's face, I see this doesn't impress her.

"Did you come here on your own?" Chloe asks, peering out a narrow window as if she expects Zobia to be lurking in the street below.

"Yes. I ran out of the house and ended up here."

"You've run away?" Her eyes widen and her lips curve in the hint of a smile.

"Not exactly. I'll have to go back of course."

She claps her hands together. "You've come for advice!"

Not wanting to disappoint her, I agree. "I guess I have."

"You want to know how to get out of this marriage with what's-his-face, the tall ugly bozo."

I nod since this is true. I do want to get out of the arranged marriage with Euphrastus.

We smile at each other like conspirators. Although younger than me, she seems more worldly. I have no doubt that she can give me advice. The gods have guided my steps to her door.

Nessa hugs her legs, head tilted, and watches us solemnly.

Chloe closes her eyes and frowns with concentration as if she has the gift of prophecy like the oracles. "He's marrying you for your inheritance, right?"

"Yes," I agree, amazed that she already knows this.

"So if you were to lose all your money . . . ?"

"It's not really mine to lose. My uncle has control of all my money until I marry."

She grimaces and tries again. Her eyes are still closed. "Suppose what's-his-face—"

"Euphrastus."

" —found out you aren't a virgin?"

I feel the blood rush to my face. "But I am."

"But suppose you weren't?"

I take a deep breath. "That would dishonor my aunt and uncle. My mother and father too even though they're gone."

She sighs and opens her eyes. "There must be something that would make him change his mind about marrying you."

"We could dye her skin blue," suggests Nessa.

Chloe giggles.

I look from one to the other. Are they serious? Blue skin might give Euphrastus pause, but my aunt and uncle would be furious. I'd get a beating for sure. And I don't think I want blue skin.

"Or she could break out in red spots," Chloe says excitedly. "An unknown disease. A curse from the gods. Highly contagious." She presses an arm dramatically to her forehead, closes her eyes, and falls back on the bed like a tragic heroine in the amphitheater.

Nessa claps her hands in delight. "Yes, let's do it."

"I could say I have the plague," I offer, hoping to avoid both blue skin and red spots.

This is met with dead silence.

"That might work," Chloe finally says, but I can tell she is just being polite.

I shouldn't have mentioned the plague. It's too real, too awful. How could I have suggested it? My family died from the plague. I can't pretend to have it just to get out of a marriage I don't want. It would be unforgivably callous.

She must see my distress on my face. "Or you may just have to marry him." She picks up her flute and blows the same mournful notes she blew that night in the courtyard.

"Chloe's in love," Nessa confides.

"I am not, you moron." Chloe snatches up a small pillow and tosses it at the younger girl. Nessa ducks and the pillow bounces harmlessly off the wall.

"I'm in love too," I tell them.

This gets their attention.

"With who?" Chloe asks. "Oh, do tell."

"The most handsome —"

"Oh, no," she interrupts. "He can't be as handsome as the boy I'm in love with. I'm in love with the most handsome boy in all of Athens."

I hesitate, remembering how we both watched Doros in the agora. Could she be in love with him too?

"Does he love you back?" I ask, my heart sinking because I can't possibly compete with Chloe. She has the delicate beauty of a nymph while I'm hopelessly ordinary.

"Are you kidding?" She rolls her eyes. "He doesn't

know I'm alive. I'm only a flute girl. What chance do I have? He could have any girl in Athens."

I try not to show my relief. Anyway, maybe it isn't Doros who has caught her eye. Maybe it's some other boy entirely.

"And you?" she asks. "This boy you love — does he love you?"

"We haven't actually spoken," I admit.

We stare at each other, then dissolve into laughter. It feels good to laugh. I laugh so hard I have tears in my eyes. Maybe that's why I don't notice the woman standing in the doorway until she speaks.

CHAPTER 11

W hat's this?"

We all look at the elegant woman in the long tunic of pale gold. She isn't a young woman. In fact, she's older than my mother or my Aunt Damaris. Nor is she beautiful, although she must have been when she was younger. Even now there is something striking about her — a commanding light in her eyes, confidence in her straight back, pride in the lift of her chin. But there are strands of grey among the black of her carefully coiffed hair and fine wrinkles at the corners of her eyes and mouth. From her air of authority, I assume she is the mistress of the house.

Chloe and Nessa exchange quick glances.

"Why aren't you practicing?" she demands.

Then her glance falls on me. "And who might you be?"

"Rhea," I reply, wishing I could vanish into thin air. I realize she may not be pleased to find a stranger in her house.

"Why are you here, Rhea?" she asks. "Don't you have a home? A mother? A father? Do your parents know where you are?" It's a barrage of questions too fast for me to answer. The last echoes in my mind. No, my parents do not know where I am.

"They're dead," I tell her bluntly. "I live with my aunt and uncle."

She looks me over. "You're an orphan?"

I think I detect a gentler note in her voice and feel encouraged. "Yes, my parents died from the plague about a month ago."

"Who is your uncle?"

"Lycurgus, son of Hippias."

Her face gives no sign of recognition. "Why are you here?"

"She came for advice," Chloe says.

The woman turns to her and raises an eyebrow. "Advice about what?"

"Marriage," Chloe answers without hesitation.

Even to my ears this sounds ludicrous.

The woman tries to restrain a smile. "And she came to you for advice? You're thirteen years old. What do you know of marriage?"

"I didn't know who else to ask," I explain, rushing to Chloe's defense. "My aunt is taking care of her sister, who has the plague, and unless I can find a way to avoid it, I'm to be married at the next full moon."

The woman turns her dark eyes back on me. They are outlined with kohl and make me feel as if a goddess is looking at me. "Why would you want to avoid it? Most girls your age are eager to marry."

"Not me," I assure her. "If I didn't have to, I'd never get married."

I can't tell if I've shocked her. She studies me thoughtfully.

"Do you expect your uncle to take care of you all your life? Wouldn't that be quite a burden for him?"

"Perhaps I could be a hetaira," I suggest, remembering the woman I met in the street. I wouldn't have dared say such a thing to my Aunt Damaris, but this woman is a stranger and that emboldens me.

"A hetaira!" she says, not sounding shocked, just mildly surprised or curious. "Would you really want such an ignoble fate? Respectable women would shun you."

"I would be a hetaira like Aspasia," I say, naming the most famous hetaira in all of Athens, the mistress of Pericles himself.

"Aspasia! And what do you know of her?"

"She's the most educated woman in all of Athens."

"That may be, but there are many who think women should not be educated."

In other circumstances I might have held my tongue, but something about her makes me want to speak up. "My father thought girls should be educated as well as boys," I tell her. If she is anything like my Aunt Damaris, this should horrify her, but even this revelation doesn't seem to faze her.

"Did he? And who was your father?"

"Theron, son of Hippias," I say, standing a little straighter.

Again she gives no sign of recognition. "And did he teach you to read and write and do sums?"

"He did." I don't care if she doesn't approve. I'm proud of my father and glad he taught me these things.

She smiles. "Where I come from, a city far across the sea, girls are taught to read. It's not like here in Athens, where they are taught only to weave and run a household."

"So can she stay?" Nessa asks hopefully. "I could teach her how to somersault."

"Of course she can't stay. She isn't a stray cat or dog. She has a home. She has relatives."

"But if she goes back," says Chloe, "she'll have to marry Euphrastus, and he's horrible."

"Euphrastus!" There is surprise in her voice, as if she recognizes the name.

Chloe hurries on without pausing for breath. "He's old and he's ugly and he has a scar running down the side of his face."

"He left his baby daughter on a mountain to die," I add. "And if I have a daughter, he may do the same to her."

She looks from Chloe to me with her dark intelligent eyes. "Why does your uncle want you to marry him?"

"My uncle owes him money, or at least that's what I've been told."

She looks upward, as if the answer to my problems is inscribed on the ceiling. I look up too but see only the intricate design of squares that covers it. "Let me think about this."

"So you'll help her?" Chloe asks.

"I'll see what I can do."

It's a neutral response. Adults always say things like that and then do nothing at all. My hopes, which have been rising, begin to fall.

"There isn't much time," I say uneasily.

She holds up a hand and her rings flash. "I'll make no promises. Now you should go home before your aunt and uncle call out the guard to search for you. Did you come alone?"

"Yes."

She frowns. "I'll send someone with you. I want you to get there safely."

I think I can get safely home by myself, but I don't want to argue with such an imperious lady, especially since she might help me. The servant she sends with me is a harmless old fellow named Nestor who looks as if he'd rather be napping in the shade of an olive tree than walking halfway across the city. I'm a bit dubious about his ability to go so far, especially since he has to lean on a walking stick, but soon enough I'm glad to have him since I'm unfamiliar with this part of the city. I ran so long without paying attention to my surroundings that it might take me a while to find my way back again. As we walk, I try to find out more about the woman I just met.

"Your mistress seems to be quite a refined and educated lady," I observe as we reach the first intersecting street.

"Oh, she is," Nestor tells me. "She's great friends with Socrates and that crowd."

I have heard of Socrates, and I know my aunt and uncle don't approve of him. People say he questions everything, even the gods.

"Just the other night Anaxagoras was at one of our banquets. You've heard of him, haven't you?"

I have. He too is a well-known philosopher. "Your master and mistress must be very important people."

"You know who she is, don't you?"

I shake my head. "No, who is she?"

"She's mistress to the most important man in Athens—Pericles himself. Surely you've heard of Aspasia?"

I feel embarrassed remembering how I stood there and told her about herself. She must have thought I was an idiot. But as I begin to recover from the shock of this discovery, I remind myself she has offered to help me. She is one of the most powerful women in Athens. If anyone can help, she can. Maybe Athena has answered my prayer after all. The thought buoys me up.

As we make our way through the narrow winding streets, I'm surprised to find that I came so far. Returning takes longer than I expected, but no doubt that's because we are walking at a snail's pace. I think I'd make better time on my own and several times politely suggest there's no need for old Nestor to trek so far, but he steadfastly refuses to abandon me.

"The streets are not safe for a young woman alone," he insists. "You should not be running around without an escort. And what would my mistress say if I failed to deliver you safely to your uncle's door?"

With a sigh I resign myself to our slow progress through the city. I doubt there is danger in the streets in broad daylight. I venture to hint as much.

"You can't be too careful," he assures me. "Just the other day a man was knifed in the agora in broad daylight."

"Really?" I say, surprised.

"And some refugees who were camped out in the Temple of Apollo were attacked by a group of ruffians."

I haven't heard about this either. It makes me wonder how many other such incidents I haven't heard about.

"These are bad times," he tells me. "Spartans burning our crops, people dying of plague." He shakes his head, as if lamenting what the world is coming to. "Who knows how it will all end."

We are near the agora now and up ahead I can see a crowd of people. My first thought is that the marketplace is busier than usual, but the old man stops in his tracks like a horse scenting danger.

"What is it?" I ask.

"I don't know, and I don't want to find out," he says, abruptly turning aside into a narrow street.

I hesitate for a fraction of a second, curious about what's happening, but I can't just abandon old Nestor after he has guided me so far. So we skirt the agora at a safe distance, making our trek longer than if we had cut through it. It is midafternoon when we finally arrive at my uncle's door.

"Won't you come in and have a glass of wine and some cheese?" I ask politely. I know he must be tired. Also Myrrine is less likely to give me a tongue lashing in front of a stranger.

"That's very kind of you, my dear," he says, "but I think I should be getting back. I don't want to be abroad when the sun sets. Too many hooligans out and about after dark."

I have no good argument for this, so I watch him turn and slowly make his way back up the street. As soon as I'm inside, Myrrine pounces.

"Where have you been? It's been hours. Why did you go running out of the house like that? Are you all right?"

I bite my lip. "Yes, of course I'm all right. I just couldn't stay in the loom room for another minute. I felt like everything was closing in on me."

She looks at me with a mixture of frustration and pity and sighs. "So where have you been?"

"Walking."

"You've been wandering about the streets all this time?"

I hesitate. "I ran into a friend."

She frowns. "What friend?"

"Chloe. She's a flute girl who lives in the Ceramicus."

"A flute girl? How do you come to be friends with a flute girl?"

"We met in the agora that day I got measured for a new pair of sandals." I don't meet her eyes. There is truth in my answer, just not the whole truth.

I start for the stairs.

"Oh, no. You come with me to the kitchen, where I can keep an eye on you."

In the kitchen she sets me to work chopping up leeks, while she kneads dough which she will bake into bread in the clay oven.

"How many times must I tell you," she says after we've been working for a few minutes. "You can't go running off like that. If your uncle finds out, you'll regret it."

"Well, he won't find out unless you tell him," I retort.

"It's dangerous out there."

"I didn't see any dangers." Then I remember the crowd in the marketplace and how old Nestor steered us clear of it. Was his instinct right to sense danger there? What was happening in the marketplace?

"Did you know a man was knifed in the agora in broad daylight?" I ask her.

She doesn't answer right away. "As I said, it's dangerous out there."

"Why didn't you tell me?"

"Your uncle thinks such things aren't appropriate for you to hear."

"What else haven't I been told?"

"Look, people aren't happy about this war—and now with the plague, they're scared."

I sigh. I'm tired of hearing about the war and the plague. "I don't see what that has to do with me," I say crossly.

"When people are angry and scared, they lash out. They don't care who they lash out at."

Maybe. But I still don't think the streets are as dangerous as she and old Nester seem to think. Nothing happened. Even if we had gone through the marketplace, probably nothing would have happened. It's ridiculous how people's imagination runs away with them, forever seeing dangers looming where there are none.

"Bad enough that you run off in the middle of the day," she continues, still not done lecturing me, "but to go visit a flute girl . . ." She shakes her head in disbelief. "You know your uncle wouldn't approve."

I told her about Chloe, but I haven't told her about Aspasia. Now I'm glad I didn't. It would just give her one more thing to scold me about. A hetaira is probably worse in her mind than a flute girl, even if that hetaira is the mistress of Pericles.

"I don't want to marry Euphrastus," I remind her.

"You don't have a choice. Get that through your head. Since when can girls choose who they'll marry?"

"He left his baby daughter on the mountainside to die!" I chop the leeks with a vengeance.

"It's a cruel world. The sooner you learn that, the better."

Cruel indeed. Forced to marry an ugly brute like Euphrastus. My family dead from the plague. She doesn't have to tell me the world is cruel. I know it only too well.

"Myrrine," I say, pausing with the knife in my hand, "have you ever been in love?"

She keeps kneading dough and doesn't meet my eyes. "What a question!"

"Well, have you?"

"Perhaps I have, perhaps I haven't. Why do you want to know?"

"I thought maybe you could give me some advice."

She glances at me warily. "You think you're in love?"

"Maybe." I can be just as evasive as she is.

"Is that why you've been sneaking out? Have you been going off to meet someone? Because if you have . . ."

"No, of course not."

She looks relieved. "Then why are you asking?"

I can't tell her about Doros. She won't ever let me out of the house again. Then a line from Sappho pops into my mind. *Blame Aphrodite.*

"I've been reading Sappho," I tell her.

She rolls her eyes. "You read too much. Your poets will put the wrong ideas into your head. Take my word for it, love is more trouble than it's worth."

"Then you *have* been in love!" I declare, triumphant to have caught her out.

I've never seen Myrrine blush before, but blush she does and looks quickly toward the open door to see if anyone has overheard.

"Who?"

"Never mind."

But I'm not going to be put off so easily. "Someone you saw in the marketplace?"

"It really doesn't matter, does it? I can't marry."

This is true. Slaves can't marry, or at least not without their master's permission, which they are unlikely to get. The irony of it hits me. There isn't much difference in our situations. Neither of us can marry who we want.

"Are you happy?" I ask.

She shrugs. "We all do what we need to do to survive. Of course I'd rather be free. Anyone would."

"Even if it meant you had to marry someone like Euphrastus?" I say, grimacing.

"Honestly, Rhea. There are worse things in this world."

"Such as?"

"Starving. Working in the silver mines. Dying of plague. Shall I go on?"

"What would you do if you were me?"

She shrugs. "I'd marry him."

Easy for her to say. She's not the one who has to marry him.

I sigh. Given the chance to trade places, I think I'd prefer to be someone's slave rather than Euphrastus's wife.

CHAPTER 12

Supper is late because Myrrine insists we wait for my uncle to come home. After an hour has passed, we give up and start without him. We are still eating when he finally arrives. Myrrine runs to meet him and apologize for starting without him. From where I sit with the other women in the courtyard, I can hear her explaining. His only reply is a curt command to send Kalchas to his study. I wonder why he wants to see Kalchas. At least it has nothing to do with me. I'm safe for a little longer. Maybe he won't find out how I ran out of the house and roamed about the streets of the Ceramicus without a chaperone.

Myrrine ducks into the dining room, where Kalchas is eating with Nikomedes. No doubt Kalchas has already heard that he's wanted in the study. When she returns to the courtyard, she has Nikomedes in tow. He doesn't look happy about joining us but sits down on one of the benches and continues chewing on a piece of bread. Myrrine looks anxious. She takes a bite of fish, then sets it down again as if no longer hungry.

"I wish the mistress would return," says Lede.

We can hear my uncle's voice rise as he talks to Kalchas.

"Sounds like Kalchas is in trouble," Lede observes.

No one else says anything. We just go on eating. Finally Nikomedes breaks the silence.

"The festival games are coming up," he says suddenly.

This too brings no response. Maybe we are all listening to hear what will come of my uncle's outburst against Kalchas.

"The athletes who are participating will be sacrificing to the gods tomorrow afternoon."

He doesn't glance at me, but I'm pretty sure this is meant for my ears. Doros is one of the athletes who will be participating. Nikomedes is letting me know it will be another chance to see him. I glance quickly around to see if anyone else understands, but no one is paying any attention. I throw him a grateful look when I finally catch his eye, then pop an olive into my mouth.

A few minutes later through the doorway I see Kalchas storm out of the study and charge into the men's sleeping room.

Nikomedes has seen him too and starts to rise.

"Finish your meal," Myrrine says quietly.

Reluctantly he sits down again. "Do you suppose it's something to do with me?" he asks.

Evidently I'm not the only one with a guilty conscience.

"Have you been doing something you shouldn't have?" Myrrine asks, fixing him with a stern look.

He stares at his half-finished meal of fish without answering. Then he jumps up and runs out of the room, ignoring her shout for him to return.

Not until later when Zobia and I are alone in our room do I find out what it was all about. It seems my uncle heard that Nikomedes had attracted the attention of a certain middle-aged man who attended some banquets at the house. He wanted to know if Kalchas had at any time taken his eyes off Nikomedes and threatened to sell him to the silver mines at Laurium if Nikomedes falls under the influence of this man. Kalchas swore he watches the boy like a hawk.

"Would he really sell him to the silver mines?" I ask, shocked at the suggestion. Kalchas has been with their family since Nikomedes was a toddler. He's practically a member of the family, just like Myrrine.

"Your uncle's not a man to cross," Zobia says, "and Nikomedes means the world to him."

I feel sorry for Kalchas and hope for his sake there is nothing to the rumor. Being sent to the silver mines is an almost certain death. However, protecting Nikomedes is an important part of his duties. Relationships between youths and older admirers are not uncommon, but it's one reason boys have pedagogues to watch them.

The next morning after breakfast Myrrine announces that she is taking me with her to fetch water from the fountain in the agora. Ordinarily I wouldn't be allowed to do this, but Damaris is not here to forbid it, and Myrrine says if I'm going to insist on leaving the house, at least this way I can make myself useful and she can keep an eye on me.

Any excuse to get out of the house is fine with me. I feel as if a weight has been lifted as we set out with our pots. The sky overhead is a perfect blue and the city is just starting to stir. It's easy to feel hopeful when the day is only beginning.

"You're very cheerful this morning," Myrrine remarks as we pass the statue of Hermes on the corner.

"Am I?"

"You were humming just now."

"I'm glad for a chance to leave the house."

"You left it only yesterday, or have you forgotten?"

"If I had my way, I'd leave it every day," I retort.

"Whatever for?"

I look at her to see if she's serious. "Don't you feel cooped up when you have to stay inside?"

She shrugs. "It makes little enough difference to me. Inside or out, there's always work to be done."

"But isn't it nicer to be out in the open where you see people around you and you can look up at the beautiful marble buildings on the hill? I feel as if I'll suffocate when I go a whole day without once going outside."

"You'd better not let your uncle hear you say that."

"I don't care if he does," I say, tossing my head.

"You will if he beats you."

"Well, he won't know unless you tell him."

"And what's to keep me from telling him what a wicked girl you are?"

"You wouldn't." I say it with confidence, fairly certain of this because Myrrine has not told him about how I ran out of the house yesterday and nobody knew where I was for hours. I'm about to thank her for not betraying me when we turn a corner and the orange tiled roof and mud-brick walls that enclose the fountain appear.

We enter the already busy structure through an open doorway. Mounted at either end are brass lion heads with water spouting from their mouths. You can dip your pot in the holding tank where the water collects or fill it directly from one of the spouts. Of course we have to wait our turn in line, but I don't mind that. It's such a lively place, full of women of all ages, both free and slave, sharing gossip and the latest news. We hear talk of who has died of the plague, whose husband or son has been called up, and a woman named Crisa who has run off with a tradesman. Then someone mentions Aspasia and Pericles. I stop listening to the other conversations to catch what is said.

"This war is their fault," a rather loud broad-backed woman ahead of us declares. "If Pericles had not insisted on fighting Sparta, we wouldn't be in this situation."

"And look at how he's let them burn our fields," says another, slimmer and younger. "He ought to have our men out there on the plains of Attica fighting them and protecting our farms."

I know what they are talking about. Not everyone agreed with Pericles that the war was necessary. Then once it was underway, instead of fighting the Spartans on land, his strategy was to bring the people from the countryside inside the city walls for protection and send ships off to fight the Spartans by sea because Athens has more and better ships. We do not depend on the countryside for our food since we can bring it in from other places by ship through our harbor at Piraeus, but of course people don't like the idea of having their fields burned and their country houses sacked. You can't blame them.

"The gods are punishing us for his arrogance," says the first woman. "This plague is his fault."

Others chime in, agreeing, and then the conversation turns back to who is ill and who has died.

When it's our turn at the spout, Myrrine and I fill our pots with water flowing from the lion's mouth. When both are full, we lift them onto our heads and start home.

"Mind you don't drop that," she warns. "Pots cost money."

"I won't drop it," I protest, annoyed that she would think me so inept.

I'm better at carrying pots on my head than I am at spinning and weaving. Like other Greek girls, I've been balancing them on my head all my life. As we walk, I gradually forget about the heavy pot on my head and mull over what we heard at the fountain.

"I don't understand why they blame Aspasia," I tell Myrrine. "I understand why they blame Pericles, but why do they blame her?"

"Because he takes advice from her. At least, that's what people say. She's a hetaira and he treats her like a wife. Better than that actually because how many men take advice from their wives? People say she even writes his speeches for him."

"Is that true?" I ask, surprised that a woman would write speeches for a man. Most women can neither read nor write.

"I have no idea. But whether it's true or not, they hold it against her."

"Well, that doesn't seem fair."

Myrrine smiles wryly. "Since when is the world fair?"

I wonder what she would say if I told her I met Aspasia yesterday. I saw how Aspasia holds herself, the way she meets the world with a bold gaze, as if she will bow to no one. Yes, Aspasia was imposing, but it's hard to imagine a woman having so much influence that she can write speeches for the most powerful man in Athens. Clearly she doesn't fit the Athenian ideal of a self-effacing and submissive wife. Athenian wives are not supposed to be active in politics and government. They are supposed to stay at home and manage their households.

"I wonder if people just dislike her because she is educated and beautiful and has caught the eye of a man like Pericles," I suggest.

"Pericles may live with her," Myrrine says, "but she will never have the Athenians' respect as his wife because he already has a wife and two legitimate sons. It doesn't matter that he left his wife and now lives with her. He can't marry her because she's a foreigner, and there are laws against Athenians marrying foreigners. She will always be a hetaira, not a wife."

Is that so terrible? At the moment I think I'd rather be a hetaira than Euphrastus's wife. Then I remember that Doros may be climbing the Acropolis this afternoon to sacrifice to the gods along with the other athletes participating in the upcoming festival games. Ever since Nikomedes mentioned that at supper last evening, I've been plotting how to get there to see them and now I have a plan.

After the pots of water have been stowed in the storage room, I run upstairs to the loom room, where Zobia is at work weaving. Fortunately I have found her alone and so I can speak openly.

"Listen, I'm going to climb the Acropolis again," I tell her, still out of breath from racing up the stairs.

She groans at the prospect of the long climb up the Great Stair.

"You don't need to come," I say hastily before she can object. "I can go alone. I'm sure I'll be quite safe."

But of course she refuses to let me go alone. "I promised your dear mother I'd look after you," she says, taking my face in her hands. "And so long as I'm able to, I shall."

Dear old Zobia! What would I do without her? Tears spring to my eyes and I give her a hug. For the rest of the morning I'm happy, knowing I may soon see Doros again.

CHAPTER 13

In midafternoon we join the crowds climbing the Great Stair. The usual throng is swollen by the ranks of boisterous young athletes laden with garlands and gifts of food for the gods. They stride past the rest of us as if we are mere plodding mortals and they are the sons of Olympus. I keep my eyes peeled for Doros.

"So are you going to tell me what this is all about?" Zobia asks as we climb.

I still haven't told her about Doros because I'm sure she wouldn't approve. But after wracking my brain, I think I've come up with an explanation that will satisfy her. She puts great store in dreams so I have concocted a dream for her.

"Last night I dreamed that I was on the Acropolis," I tell her, "and Artemis was standing there, an olive branch in her hand." The olive tree is sacred to Athena, so it's not surprising that she would be holding an olive branch in my dream. The olive branch is a nice touch and I'm proud of it.

"Oh, an olive branch, was it?"

I ignore the sarcasm in her voice and continue.

"Yes, and I think it means if I go there, something will happen, and then I won't have to marry Euphrastus."

"Is that so? Well, I think your dream means you should put aside all this stubbornness and face what's coming. The sooner you start accepting your destiny, the better."

"I'll never accept it if it means marrying Euphrastus. I'll run away before I become his wife."

"You will do no such thing. Where would you go?"

"I could leave Athens," I suggest, remembering my conversation with Maron in the cemetery.

"And go where?"

"There are lots of places I could go."

"And how would you live? Have you thought about that?"

"I don't know," I admit. "Maybe I'd write poems — like Sappho."

"Sappho wasn't an orphan."

True. Sappho was not at the mercy of an aunt and uncle intent on marrying her off to a horrid brute of a man. Well, soon Aspasia will fix it so that I won't have to marry Euphrastus. And then maybe I can live at her house in the Ceramicus with Chloe and Nessa. Maybe I can even take Zobia with me. This plan seems so perfect that my heart feels lighter for the rest of the climb and I ignore everything Zobia says about how my scrolls have filled my head with foolish ideas. She is my rock, but what does she know of poetry and the yearnings of a young woman's heart?

Once we reach the top, we pass through the great

colonnaded gateway and then I pause to look at the hordes of people around us. There are always crowds on the Acropolis. Most people come to the temples to offer sacrifices to the gods, but there are also those who have business at the treasury, and now with the war on, there are also people from the countryside who have no place to go and are taking refuge in the temples.

"Now what?" Zobia says, looking about. "Do you see the goddess?"

"Of course not. She won't show herself until she's ready." Clearly Zobia does not believe my story of a prophetic dream, but it's too late now to invent another. I wonder how I'm going to persuade her to be patient until I see Doros. I just hope we haven't already missed him.

"Isn't that the sculptor we met here last time?" She squints in the direction of the little temple of Athena Nike, where we sheltered from the rain. I look, and indeed there is Maron, talking to a young man as they both look up at the frieze above their heads.

"He isn't why you wanted to come here, is he?" she asks suspiciously.

I throw her a wounded look. "Of course not. Why would you think that?"

"Because you were entirely too friendly with him the last time we were here."

"I was not," I object. "I was just being polite."

"Well, you're not supposed to be polite to young men you don't know."

"Oh, I'm to be rude, am I?"

"You're not supposed to be anything at all. Proper young women should be neither seen nor heard."

Just then Maron looks up and sees us. He waves. Since I can as easily watch for Doros from the little temple as from anywhere else, I start walking in that direction. Zobia, muttering her objections, follows me.

"What are you doing?" I ask when I reach Maron.

"Working, as you can see. I've got an apprentice today to keep an eye on. What about you? I see you've got your shadow." He flashes a smile at Zobia, who with a groan is settling herself on the temple steps. I don't think she noticed. Or maybe she is ignoring him. In any case her disapproval could not be more obvious.

"I came to make a sacrifice to the goddess," I tell him, holding up the cloth in which my honey cakes are wrapped.

"Again? Are you sure you didn't come to see me?"

I feel the blood rush to my face. Having little experience of young men, I'm not used to such remarks. It seems impertinent, especially for a slave, but I don't want Maron to think I'm unfriendly or easily take offence. "I thought you were working on a stele in the cemetery," I say to hide my confusion.

"I finished that, although there's been brisk work there lately, what with the plague. I can make a few drachmas on the side. Eventually I'll be able to buy my freedom."

"And then you'll leave Athens?" I ask, remembering our conversation in the cemetery. I feel a twinge of envy when I imagine him traveling abroad. His future seems so much rosier than mine.

He shrugs. "I might stay. There's plenty of work here for a sculptor, unless of course the Spartans take over. They've much less use for sculptors than the Athenians."

Sparta, it's true, is not known for its architecture or monuments. Compared to Athens, it's a very unremarkable city of plain buildings and squat temples. The Spartans don't see this as a failing. They think beauty is an unnecessary luxury and pride themselves on the austerity of their city and their lives. But like all Athenians, I'm sure I'd much rather live in Athens.

"It's very busy here today," I say, stepping aside as several young men stampede past me on their way to the altar.

"It's because of the games tomorrow," Maron says, squinting in the sunlight. "The athletes who will participate are making the rounds of the city, sacrificing and offering up bribes to Hercules, Nike, and any other gods or goddesses they think might help them win. The temple altars will be heaped today."

We watch as the young men lay flowers, berries, and honey cakes on the altar and then rush off whooping to the next temple. An old man whom they nearly knock over shouts after them to be more respectful.

"As if the gods care," Maron murmurs.

"Of course they do," I say, mildly shocked he would speak so slightingly of the gods in this sacred place.

"I suppose you believe in the gods?" He looks at me with one brow raised.

"Of course I do." I glance around furtively, hoping he has not been overheard. The punishment for impiety can be severe—whipping or even death. He should be more careful what he says in public regardless of what he thinks privately.

His apprentice, a skinny curly-haired young man, has climbed the scaffolding and is diligently chipping away at the half-finished frieze. Either he's so intent on his work that he didn't hear Maron's remark, or he's politely pretending not to have heard.

"They are just stories," Maron says. "Surely you must realize that. The Greeks have their gods, just like the Persians and Egyptians have theirs. What makes you think the Greek gods are any more real than those of the Persians or Egyptians? Or do you believe in their gods too?"

"Of course not. The Persians and Egyptians are barbarians."

"Are they?" He seems amused by my response.

I don't see why he finds that funny. "Everyone knows Greece is the most civilized country in the world," I add.

"Do they? And does that go for the slaves sweating in the silver mines?"

This seems to me unfair. "What other people have such noble temples and monuments, poets and athletes, philosophers and statesmen?" I demand.

My eyes are drawn to the Great Stair below us swarming with people. Beyond lies the city with its orange tiled roofs, stately buildings, columns, statues, and shady trees. In the distance is Piraeus with its harbor and the blue of the Saronic Gulf.

"I admit it has beauty," he says quietly, "but the gods are just stories."

Thank goodness Zobia isn't sitting close enough to hear. She would be scandalized. But I'm more open-minded. I don't agree with him, but I will allow him his opinion.

"So have you managed to get out of that arranged marriage yet?" he asks.

"No, but I found someone who can help me." I feel relieved the topic has changed.

"Not a god?"

I ignore this. "Someone important."

He looks down at the Great Stair. "So you won't have to marry your suitor after all?"

"I hope not."

"But you're not sure?"

I glance at Zobia. She's not looking at us, but I suspect she's watching us out of the corner of her eye.

"How long before the nuptials if you don't manage to stop them?" he asks.

"A month." I bite my lip.

"That's not much time."

As if I don't know that.

"You deserve better," he says. "Forcing you to marry a man you don't want to marry is a barbaric custom."

I blink. I've never thought of it like that. All over Athens, parents and guardians choose the men their daughters will marry, and their daughters' desires are seldom taken into account. This is the way it's been done for generations and no doubt will be for generations to come. It's regrettable, but *barbaric*?

I would argue the point, but just then I catch sight of Doros approaching the temple with a group of boys, flushed from the climb up the Great Stair, muscular and beautiful. I quickly look away so no one will notice me staring, but not so quickly that Maron misses it.

"Someone you know?"

I could pretend not to understand, but I suspect my face has already given me away. "No, I mean, yes. That is, he's a friend of my cousin's." Could I have tripped over my tongue any more badly?

"He's a good-looking boy," Maron says thoughtfully.

My face feels hot. I hope Doros and his friends can't hear him. I should not have come over to talk to Maron. It was a mistake.

"That's him, isn't it?" Maron says. "The boy you told me about. The reason you came to the temple that day we met."

I don't know what to say. Explanations race through my mind. None of them very convincing.

"He can't be more than seventeen."

I could point out to him that I'm only fifteen. Yet I'm old enough to be married. And Doros is almost old enough to go to war.

"Does he know how you feel?"

I want to run away, but I'm afraid that might make Doros and his friends notice me, and I don't want to be noticed. If I stand very still, maybe I will be invisible. *Athena Nike, if you are there, please hide me . . .*

"I'll take that for a no," Maron says. "Perhaps I should call him over."

"No!" I'm horrified. He wouldn't, would he?

"That's why you're here, isn't it? You didn't come to make an offering to the goddess. You came hoping to see him."

"Could you please lower your voice?" I beg, my face burning.

Maron doesn't appear to hear me. "What's his name?"

I close my eyes, wondering how I got myself into such an awkward situation. "Doros," I whisper. Just saying his name aloud makes my heart beat faster. I open my eyes.

To my relief the boys are leaving. There are five of them, noisy and high-spirited, good-naturedly jostling each other. Doros is in the middle. For a fraction of a second his eyes meet mine as he passes. Eyes as blue as the Aegean. I stand as still as a statue, hardly daring to breathe.

Zobia is standing now, frowning at me in disapproval, but I don't mind. Now nothing else matters. I've seen Doros, and he's seen me. We haven't actually spoken, but we've looked into each other's eyes. I feel breathless and my heart is pounding.

Maron looks pensive as he watches them bound away.

"I have to go," I say.

"Wait." He touches my arm and I stop, startled by this familiarity. "Tell me. Who will help you get out of marrying Euphrastus? You were telling the truth about that, right?"

"Of course I was."

"Because I heard something about him—something bad. I don't think you should marry him."

That makes two of us. I wonder what he's heard, but Zobia is scowling at me and there's no time to ask. "Aspasia," I say and see the look of surprise on his face. I run up to the altar and lay my offering of honey cake next to the flowers and silver coins left by the young athletes. Then, without another glance at Maron, I join Zobia.

CHAPTER 14

The sooner you're married, the better," Zobia declares as we walk away from the temple of Athena Nike.

"How can you say that?" I demand. "You know how I hate the idea of marrying Euphrastus."

"Do you think I don't have eyes to see? I may be getting old, but I was young once and I remember what it's like to fall in love."

I roll my eyes. I can't remember a time when Zobia wasn't old.

"I don't know what you're talking about."

"Oh, you don't? You think I didn't notice back there at the little temple?"

I feel myself flushing again. Was I so obvious? Does she know about Doros?

"You have to forget about him. You'll be a married woman soon. You can't go around mooning over young men you meet in the street. It isn't respectable."

"I don't care."

"You'd better care. Virtue once lost is lost forever."

I sigh. How many times have I heard that? "And anyway I may not have to marry Euphrastus after all."

This gets her attention. "What do you mean?"

I have told her about meeting Aspasia but not about how I asked Aspasia for help. Now it tumbles out as we stand there in front of the Parthenon surrounded by hordes of people.

"She said she would help you?" There is disbelief in her voice. "Are you sure that's what she said?"

"Yes, of course I'm sure." I feel annoyed that she should doubt me.

"They say she has the ear of Pericles, but still—I don't see how she could help you. What could she possibly do? Don't get your hopes up, child. And you need to forget about this young man. Even if your aunt and uncle had not already chosen your husband, they wouldn't choose him."

I know that, but can I help it if the god of love has pierced my breast with one of his arrows? Who can withstand that? Not even mighty Apollo was able to avoid its bittersweet sting.

"No matter how handsome he is," Zobia says, "the fact remains that he's a slave, and you're freeborn."

Now it's my turn to stare at her. Doros isn't a slave. What's she talking about? Then I realize she means Maron. "You think I'm in love with Maron?" I ask incredulously. I clap a hand over my mouth to keep from laughing. "He's just a friend, sort of like a big brother, like Jason."

"That doesn't change the fact that he's a slave. Your uncle would never approve."

"But you can't think I'm in love with him." I'm amazed that she has so completely misunderstood.

"I don't see why that's so funny," she says stiffly. "You two seem to have plenty to talk about, considering you barely know him. And there must be some reason you want to climb up here. I doubt it's for the view, and if you think you're going to pull the wool over my eyes with a silly story about a dream, you're much mistaken."

I can't believe she has gotten it so wrong. But in any case, my secret is still safe. She has no clue about my feelings for Doros. Then as if my thoughts have summoned him, he and his friends emerge from between the pillars of the old temple of the gods. At sight of him, my heart beats faster. So Psyche must have felt when she gazed for the first time on the sleeping Eros. Everything around me falls away.

A girl's lilting voice startles me from my reverie: "Look who's here."

Chloe is walking toward me in a pale blue tunic and mantle with a chaperone at her side. I feel torn between wanting to watch Doros and wanting to greet Chloe. We hug each other like old friends.

Her chaperone, an unattractive woman with coal black brows, barely raises her eyes from the ground to look at me. She and Zobia exchange mistrustful glances.

"Are you here to make an offering or to check out the athletes?" Chloe asks in a voice pitched low enough to elude Zobia's ears.

I feel the blood rush to my face. Doros and his friends are headed back toward the Parthenon.

"Never mind," she says, linking arms with me. "There's

no reason we can't do both." Her eyes sweep the crowd. "Have you ever seen so many chiseled torsos in one place outside of the Street of Statues?"

I'm sure I'm crimson now. I glance around to see if anyone has overheard. I don't think they have, although Zobia is watching us closely.

"I know why you're here," Chloe murmurs.

"And I know why you're here," I murmur back, remembering that she too is in love. "Have you seen him?" I mean the boy who has caught her eye. I just hope it's not Doros. Now where did he disappear to? Ah, yes, there he is, on the steps of the Parthenon.

"Perhaps. And you?"

"I have."

She squeezes my hand. "So why are you standing about here? Aren't you afraid some other girl may snap him up?"

"He's with his friends."

"Aren't they all?" She rolls her eyes.

"What would you do?"

She grins. "I'd bump into him" — she bumps against my hip to demonstrate — "but I'd make him think he bumped into me and while he was apologizing I'd introduce myself."

I know I could never be this bold. I'd die of embarrassment.

"And then I'd ask him if he's going to compete tomorrow. And since all men, young and old, love to talk about themselves, he'd start telling me about himself."

I'm impressed by how much she knows about men. No doubt she has learned it from her experience performing at banquets. I doubt I will ever be as knowledgeable.

"What about your chaperone?" I ask, glancing at the black-browed woman with the anxious expression.

"Phylia? What about her?"

"She doesn't mind your striking up a conversation with a young man?"

"Well, how is she going to stop me?"

I glance again at Phylia's anxious face and the way her eyes dart about the crowd as if danger lurks everywhere. I too doubt she could stop Chloe from doing as she pleased. Zobia, on the other hand, won't let me out of her sight for a minute, so I have no hope of getting close enough to Doros to bump against him or start a conversation even if I were to get up the nerve.

As if reading my mind, Zobia tugs at my arm, signaling that it's time to go. It seems like we only just got here. I glance around, trying to catch another glimpse of Doros. There are many young men and boys about, but no sign of him.

"Are you coming to visit me again soon?" Chloe asks.

"I don't know if I can."

"Run away, like you did that day," she whispers in my ear.

Zobia tugs again, more impatiently.

"Sorry. I can't stay longer," I tell Chloe.

"Never mind," she says. "We'll see each other again soon. I feel certain of it. And now there are sights to see, gods who are waiting, and we have only a short while to enjoy it all. Right, Phylia?"

Phylia looks unhappy and clutches her mantle tighter around her head.

Zobia frowns as they walk away. "Wasn't that the young woman from the agora the other day?"

"It was," I say.

"The one who works for Aspasia?"

"Yes."

"Didn't you say she's a flute girl?"

"So?"

She shakes her head. "This is what comes of running about. Flute girls and sculptor-slaves."

"I don't care," I say, lifting my chin. "They're my friends."

"Friends? A girl your age shouldn't have friends."

I ignore her. If everyone had their way, I would never leave the house or meet anybody. I don't care if Chloe is a flute girl and Maron a slave. Does that mean we can't be friends?

Not until we are descending the Great Stair, do I wonder what Maron heard about Euphrastus. I wish I had stayed and asked what it was, but seeing Doros and Chloe swept everything else out of my mind. I could run back and ask Maron, but I don't want him to think I'm forward, although surely he understands we can be no more than friends. Zobia is right. He's a slave. My uncle would not only beat me for such an alliance; he might even sell me into slavery. I heard that happened once to a girl who defied her parents and ran off with a slave. It just isn't done, or you have to be willing to sacrifice everything—your family, your freedom, the freedom of your unborn children. I don't think I could do that. And anyway I'm not in love with Maron. I'm in love with Doros.

CHAPTER 15

There may be a war on and plague spreading through the city, but that doesn't stop the festival games from taking place as usual. The city is charged with excitement. If only I could be out in the streets, cheering the runners on, but young unmarried women aren't supposed to attend, and so unfortunately I must stay at home, waiting to hear who won. Time creeps by, and I wander from the loom room upstairs to the courtyard downstairs so many times that Zobia loses patience and scolds me for my restlessness. Not until Nikomedes and Kalchas return in the late afternoon do I hear that Doros has won the footrace. I can hardly hide my joy. In my mind I see him crowned with an olive wreath and borne aloft on the shoulders of his friends. What a sight it must have been! If only I could have been there!

Then, as if those few short hours of respite have drawn the attention of a spiteful god, calamity befalls us. A messenger arrives at dusk with word that Damaris's sister has died. There is little time for mourning because laws decree that the body of a plague victim must be disposed of quickly. So early the following morning we have a hastily arranged pre-dawn procession by torchlight to the cemetery just outside the city wall by the Dipylon Gate. Dressed in black, we sing funeral dirges and wail. When it's over, Damaris takes to her bed, ill with fever and chills. We tiptoe around the house, forbidden to enter the room where she lies, attended only by Merope. Poor Merope! Her eyes are red and swollen from crying. She has to eat alone and the other slaves shun her for fear of catching the plague. Lycurgus flees the house early in the morning and doesn't return until after dark. He goes out again in the evening, as if he can't bear being under the roof where his wife lies ill.

It is during this trying time that old Xantippe, who before seldom left her bed, gets up and begins to wander. At first she just roams about the house and we find her in odd places like the men's sleeping quarters, or in the courtyard in the middle of the night. Then she begins to wander out into the streets and we have to go in search of her.

We don't know where she thinks she's going or what she's looking for on these nighttime rambles. It's impossible to know what she's thinking. She has taken to calling me Nysa, the name of a slave who served her family when she was young. She talks to me for hours about people now dead and gone as if she saw them only yesterday. I listen but it's as if we inhabit different worlds. I don't understand hers and she doesn't understand mine. I wonder where she is trying to go when she slips out the door, but there seems no pattern to her wanderings. One night she heads for the agora and the next for the Dipylon Gate, as if she intends to visit the cemetery or leave the city. The night after that she makes it to the Law Court. Wherever we find her, afterward she allows herself to be led docilely home like a child when playtime is done.

Meanwhile, Damaris's condition rapidly worsens. We can hear her moans throughout the house day and night. It's torture to listen to her.

"Will she die?" I ask Zobia on the fourth night as I lie awake listening to the faint moans rise from the downstairs room where Damaris has been moved because it's easier to care for her there.

"It's in the hands of the gods," Zobia says. "Pray to Apollo."

I do, but I doubt it will do any good. Like Athena, the god of light and healing seems to have turned his back on us.

I regret that I haven't tried harder to please my aunt. She's a good woman and was only trying to do what she thought was right when she and my uncle arranged a marriage for me. We haven't been close, but I feel sorry for her now. She doesn't deserve to suffer so. No one does.

On the fifth day of my aunt's illness, Merope runs away. It takes us several hours to notice she is gone. No one saw her at breakfast, but it's not until about noon when Damaris's cries for water grow more insistent that we realize Merope is missing.

Lycurgus is away, so it falls to the women—Myrrine,

Zobia, and Lede—to figure out what to do. No one wants to enter the sick room, which could mean being the next to catch the plague. After much arguing, they agree to draw lots. Lede loses. She accepts her bad luck stony-faced and at once sets about filling a cup with water to carry to her ailing mistress.

After eight days of illness Damaris dies. Once again the funeral rites must be performed without delay. Lycurgus holds up stoically during the pre-dawn procession to the cemetery but breaks down weeping as he pours the libation over his wife's grave. A stone's throw away another burial is taking place, more torches burning in the night, more wailing and crying, more shadowy figures wavering like shades in Hades. In spite of my mantle I can't stop shivering. Why are the gods making us suffer so? What have we done to deserve so much misery? How many more will die before it ends?

Later, after the house has been purified to rid it of the pollution brought by a death within its walls, we go about our usual tasks with heavy hearts. So far Lede shows no signs of plague—no fever or chills, no headache or stomach pains, no skin rash, no burning thirst. She sacrifices zealously to the household gods and to Apollo and his son Asclepius, god of healing. We all hold our breath, including Lede, hoping there will be no more victims of plague in the household.

Lycurgus disappears during the day. When he comes home in the evening, he reeks of wine and is in a bad temper. In the loom room Zobia scolds Lede when she brings it up and reminds her that he is grieving for Damaris.

Two days after the funeral I'm about to enter the loom room when I hear Lede say, "He's gambling again, mark my words. I'll wager he's no stranger in the brothels of the Ceramicus either."

"Watch your tongue," says Myrrine with a swift look at me.

Lifting her eyes, Lede sees me standing in the doorway and closes her mouth tightly.

These are things I'm not supposed to hear, but I'm a child no longer. I live in a city wracked by war and decimated by plague. I only have to look about me to know that life is fragile. It seems as if the city is falling apart. In the next street thieves broke into a house and stole valuables. In the Street of Statues two men were attacked on their way home from a banquet and robbed of their cloaks and purses. Nearly every night we hear drunken revelers in the streets singing on their way home from banquets.

Life has always been a gift from the gods that can be snatched away at any time. The poets tell us this. But while the warrior can die on the battlefield and such death brings glory, there is no glory in dying of plague. It has already taken so many and shows no signs of abating. No one can remember a pestilence as bad as this one. Nothing seems to stop it — not sacrificing to the gods, not amulets, not physicians. Wealthy people wonder what good their wealth is if it can't save them from the plague so they spend recklessly on temporary pleasures and material goods, or like my uncle, gamble. Poor people think they have little to lose so they turn to thieving, and the Scythian archers, charged with keeping the peace, are kept busy as crime escalates.

In addition to all this, every day brings me closer to my dreaded marriage to Euphrastus and still no word from Aspasia. My desperation is growing. To stay cooped up in the house like a prisoner seems at times intolerable. So one night I decide to sneak out. Perhaps old Xantippe has given me this idea. If an old woman can roam the streets at night, why not me?

I arrange my bedding so that Zobia, waking in the night and glancing at my bed, will think she sees me lying there. Then I wait until the household is asleep before stealing down the stairs. My heart thumps wildly in my chest as I close the door behind me. I pause a moment to look about me. Everything seems different at night. The walls of the houses gleam palely in the moonlight; stars are strewn across the night sky as if Demeter has been sowing celestial seeds. It's beautiful but scary too. My heart beats faster at the thought of all the dangers of the night—drunken revelers on their way to their next banquet, thieves prowling the streets for victims to rob, and ruffians looking for mischief under the cover of dark. But none of these deters me.

I've never been out alone in the city at night before. Always I was with others—in torchlight processions to the cemetery or searches for old Xantippe. This time I'm alone and there are no torches, but the moon is bright and the night sky cloudless and full of stars that light my way. At first my plan is to walk to the agora and back, but when I reach the nearly deserted agora without incident, I have the urge to go farther. Not too far away is the amphitheater, and the thought of seeing it in the moonlight spurs me on.

Built on the southern slope of the Acropolis, the

amphitheater juts out from the hillside. I have been there before with my family for the play competitions at the festival of Dionysus. Like other families, we brought along a picnic lunch and cushions to sit on the hard stone seats. The stories acted out on the stage before us by the masked actors were sometimes terrifying and sometimes hilarious. They were familiar stories of the gods and men, but seeing them brought to life on the stage made them new and strange, and though I knew what would happen—that Orpheus would lose Eurydice, that Medea would kill her children, that Theseus would slay the Minotaur and find his way out of the labyrinth—still I held my breath and wondered what would happen.

On this night as I draw near, the walls of the amphitheater rise starkly before me. My heart beats faster as I step through the gateway. To my surprise, I'm not alone. A small band of refugees have set up camp in the proscenium, where the plays are performed. I hesitate, but when they pay no attention to me, I grow braver and begin to climb the tiers of stone seats. I decide to climb to the top, which I have never done before but which I always wanted to do when I was a child. It feels exhilarating to climb, as if I'm moving farther away from my problems with every step. Not until I'm near the top do I realize I'm not alone here either. There is a man sitting in the dark on the highest tier—a shadowy figure, inky black on black.

CHAPTER 16

All my aunt's warnings about the dangers of the city come rushing back. Perhaps the man before me is a thief or a murderer. I'm a long way from the refugees encamped below, and if he attacks me, there's no one to come to my aid. How foolish I was to take this risk! My heart pounds in my chest so loudly I wonder if he can hear it.

As I debate what to do, he stands and the moonlight falls on his face. With a shock I recognize Maron.

"Rhea!" he exclaims, sounding equally surprised to see me.

Relieved, I clamber up the remaining tier of seats and join him. At this moment there's no one else I'd rather see.

"What are you doing here?" he asks, looking back the way I've come. "You aren't alone, are you?"

"What are *you* doing here?" I counter.

"Is your family crazy — letting you run about the city at night without even a household slave for protection?"

"They don't know I'm here," I admit, disappointed that he doesn't seem as pleased to see me as I am to see him.

"It isn't safe. You shouldn't be roaming the streets alone."

He sounds as tiresome as Zobia. I was not expecting a scolding.

"I got here unharmed, didn't I?"

"Don't you know there are all sorts of dangerous people out there on the streets? You could be beat up, or worse."

I roll my eyes. But he isn't ready to let it go.

"What if it had been someone else up here and not me? Do you value your life so little?"

I don't feel like being lectured. I get enough of that from Zobia and Myrrine. Why does everyone treat me as if I'm a child? It's bad enough that Zobia and Myrrine do it. I'm not going to take if from Maron too. Of course I value my life. How could I not after losing my family to the plague? Surely he must realize that. And then I remember that he doesn't know about Damaris.

"My aunt died," I inform him, as if that explains why I am there. All my lightheartedness falls away as I remember that she is gone.

He stares at me. "Oh god, Rhea, I'm sorry. I didn't know. When did that happen?"

"Four days ago."

He sits down again on the stone bench, and I sit beside him. The stone feels cold through my clothes and I shiver.

"I'm tired of being closed in by walls," I tell him. "I'm tired of never being able to walk along a street in the dark or look up at the night sky like this. Yes, I can sneak down to the courtyard, but it's not the same. Not a whole sky full of stars overhead like this. You're a slave, but your master lets you go wherever you want. You're more free than I am."

Maron shakes his head. "He doesn't let me go wherever I want. He's mostly interested in whether I'm earning my keep, and so long as I am, he doesn't complain."

"So why are you here?" I gesture at the amphitheater spread out around us.

He shrugs. "I come here sometimes when I want to be alone and think."

"What do you think about?"

"Life." He looks up at the sky above us, which is dusted with stars as far as the eye can see.

"Are you cold?" he asks.

"No." I try not to shiver. "Do you live near here?"

He looks sideways at me. "Why do you want to know?"

"Just curious."

"I live in the Ceramicus on the Street of Potters. There are fifteen of us—sculptors, masons, and apprentices. Not much privacy."

"That day I saw you at the temple of Nike . . . "

"What about it? "

"You said you heard something bad about Euphrastus."

"Well, it doesn't matter now, does it, since you're not going to marry him? That's what you said, right? You said Aspasia is going to help you. Or were you just making that up?"

"I wasn't making it up," I say, hurt that he would doubt me. "She did say she would help me. But tell me what you heard about him."

He hesitates. "It could be just a rumor."

"What was it?"

"I heard he killed a man."

Another shiver runs through me. This time it has nothing to do with the cool night air or the cold stone seat. I see again the cruel scar running down the side of Euphrastus's face like a portent. "Do you think it's true?"

"I don't know. Maybe."

I feel a prickle of fear. My parents would never have expected me to marry a man like Euphrastus, but who can I turn to for help now? My uncle is so consumed by his grief that he's blind to all else, and even before my aunt died, he was unwilling to listen to me. How much more so now. Aspasia said she would help me, but I haven't heard from her and time is running out.

"How sure are you that she'll help you?" he asks, as if he can guess my thoughts.

"She will. She has to!"

"Did you know that there's to be a vote at the Assembly on whether to let Pericles continue as General?"

I recall the gossip of the women at the fountain in the agora. I know people blame Pericles for the war and the plague, but I didn't know there would be a vote. Maron doesn't have to explain that if the people vote against him, it will strip him of his power and then Aspasia may not be able to help me. I feel a tightness in my chest and throat as I see my one hope for a reprieve slipping away.

"You've got to talk to her," Maron says firmly. "If you wait, it may be too late."

I nod. He's right. I should go to her as soon as possible. Before it's too late.

"Have you tried to talk to your uncle? Maybe if you tell him how you feel . . ."

I shake my head. "He won't listen."

"There must be something you can do."

I look up at the night sky again. So vast, so beautiful, so timeless. I understand why Maron comes here to think. Homer and Sappho and all the poets before them looked up at the stars like this. Human problems dwarf in comparison. In a thousand years it won't matter if I married Euphrastus or not. However, that's not much consolation.

"I wish I could help you," he says.

But of course he can't. It's late. I'd like to stay, but I ought to be getting back.

"You're leaving already?" he asks as I rise.

"Yes, I should go back now before anyone notices I'm gone."

"I'll come with you."

This time I don't protest. In fact I'm glad to have his company. With Maron beside me I feel safe. I don't have to worry about carousers stumbling home from a banquet.

As we walk back through the moonlit streets of Athens, Maron points out columns of temples, friezes, and statues we pass, and although I have seen them before, it's like I'm seeing them for the first time. I'm amazed by how well he knows the city. Through his eyes it becomes a veritable Olympus worthy of the gods in the splendor of its architecture. I think I'll never look at it quite the same again. As we near my uncle's house, I find myself wishing that our walk didn't have to end.

"By the way, don't come looking for me in the Street of the Potters," he warns.

"I suppose you're going to tell me it's too dangerous."

"Well, it is."

Somewhere an owl hoots, a lonesome but beautiful sound. Some people think that's a bad omen, but I've always liked it.

"I worry about you," Maron says as the wall of my uncle's house looms beside us.

I grimace. "You sound like Zobia. You aren't superstitious, are you?" I assume it's the hoot of the owl which made him say that.

Suddenly he cups my face in his hands and kisses me. It happens so fast it's over before I can react. I stare at him, surprised.

"Sorry," he says. "I shouldn't have done that."

He's absolutely right. He shouldn't have. I'm at a loss for words. Our friendship has just gone from simple to very complicated. I don't want to hurt his feelings, but I mustn't let him think I wanted him to kiss me. I didn't, did I? I'm not sure. I feel as if I should explain. "I like you, Maron, but surely you understand . . ." The rest of the sentence won't come.

"I understand," he says bitterly. "I'm a slave."

"That's not it at all," I protest.

"Let's just forget this happened. I don't know what I was thinking."

He turns abruptly and walks away without looking back. I don't want to part like this. What if he never speaks to me again? I don't want to lose his friendship. Oh, why does everything have to be so complicated?

CHAPTER 17

I have to go out today," I tell Zobia the next morning after I have tied my belt about my waist and tied my hair back. We are still in the small room we share. The early morning light drifts in through a narrow window.

"And why must you go out?" she asks, pinning her hair up in a neat coil.

"To see Aspasia."

She frowns. "What if your uncle finds out?"

"I hope he won't."

She looks unhappy. "I'm sure a great lady like Aspasia has far more important things to think about. You shouldn't be bothering her with your problems."

"I have to see her," I insist, determined not to let Zobia talk me out of it. "Time is running out. Who else can help me?" I catch her hands. "Please. You know what this means to me. I can't marry Euphrastus."

She sighs and relents. "All right. We'll go to see her, but

not before midday. A lady of means like Aspasia no doubt lies abed in the morning. It would be rude for us to show up too early."

I'm impatient to set out, but she is probably right, and I don't want to upset Aspasia when so much depends on her. Reluctantly I agree to wait until midday.

The morning passes so slowly it seems as if it will never come to an end. I try not to think about Maron as I wind strands of wool around the spindle, but try as I might, I can't help thinking about the previous evening, especially the kiss. I can still feel the sudden touch of his hands on my face and his lips against mine. I should have prevented it from happening. And afterward I should have explained myself better. I fear it will make things awkward now between us.

When the sun reaches its zenith, Zobia and I set off on our trek through the maze of Athens' streets. At this time of day they are full of carts and people, as if all the city is in motion. Aspasia's house is farther than I remember and several times I think we are lost, but at last we find our way to the narrow street with the crowded houses. This time there is no sound of a flute, just a baby crying somewhere and a small dog barking. I knock at the door and it's opened after a few minutes by a slave. I give her my name and ask to see Aspasia. The woman leaves us standing there while she goes in search of her mistress. Soon she is back and invites us to enter, indicating a bench where we can sit. Zobia looks down at the colorful mosaic on the floor, then up at the coffered ceiling, and finally at a marble statue of a nymph standing on a nearby pedestal. After several minutes Aspasia appears in a long blue tunic, a gold ornament tucked in her black hair.

"Rhea," she says, holding her hands out to me, "how nice to see you again. I'm afraid Chloe and Nessa are not here. I had to send them away for a while."

"I didn't come to see Chloe and Nessa," I tell her. "I came to see you."

She glances at Zobia, then back toward the wide arched doorway behind her, which leads into the recesses of the house.

"You said you could help me," I remind her.

"I said I would see what I could do," she corrects me. "Unfortunately it seems I can do nothing."

"No!"

Zobia lays a restraining hand on my arm.

"I'm sorry," Aspasia says. "There's nothing I can do."

"But you said —"

"Child, we don't always get what we want."

I struggle to hold back my tears. My disappointment is acute. I pinned all my hopes on her. She was supposed to save me from this terrible marriage. I feel as if the earth just opened under me.

"When you were here before," she explains, "I thought I might be able to arrange for your prospective husband to be called up for duty."

Hope revives at her words. Yes, that would be perfect. Called up for duty, Euphrastus might have to leave so fast there would be no time for a wedding, and he might be gone for months, or not return at all. Not that I wish for him to die. I just don't want to marry him.

"But now —" She breaks off with a wave of her hand that suggests the futility of this plan and again glances at the doorway. I sense that someone is waiting for her in one of the rooms that lay beyond, perhaps Pericles himself.

"Is it because of the vote?" I ask, remembering what Maron had said about how there would be a vote to see if Pericles continued as leader.

Again Zobia touches my arm, reminding me of my place, but I want to know.

Aspasia's face darkens with anger, but it is not me she is angry at. "Stupid little men. After all he's done for this city, they should be grateful." She shakes her head. "If only that were all. Perhaps you've heard he lost his two sons recently to the plague?"

"Yes." I know she is referring to his sons by his wife, both young men with their lives before them. The whole city knows how grief-stricken Pericles is by the loss of his sons, as any father would be.

"Well, now it's his turn."

It takes me a few seconds to grasp her meaning. Then I understand. Pericles has the plague. I look in alarm at the doorway. Is he in one of the other rooms? I hear Zobia's quick intake of breath as she reaches the same conclusion.

"You shouldn't be here," Aspasia says wearily. "There is plague in this house. That's why I sent Chloe and Nessa away — to keep them safe. But maybe there's no place left in Athens which is safe." She sounds defeated.

"I'm sorry." I stand to leave because there is nothing else that she can do for us or that we can do for her. Beside me Zobia has scrambled to her feet, clutching her mantle about her as if it will protect her from the contagion.

"I'm sorry too," Aspasia says. "I would have liked to

help you. You seem like a sweet girl. It pains me to see you forced to marry a man like Euphrastus."

"I heard he murdered a man," I tell her.

"I heard that too," she says, looking at me with sad eyes.

"Is it true?"

She shrugs. "Who knows? Sometimes things happen and witnesses are few or it's dark. Sometimes money changes hands. It's a shame the dead can't tell us how they die." She takes my hands in hers again. "May the gods protect you."

"And you as well," I say. We all three know the risk she is taking by nursing Pericles. She could catch the plague and die. I think she is very brave. And I think she must love him very much.

CHAPTER 18

As we retrace our steps through the winding streets, the hopelessness of my situation is borne down on me. I could try talking to my uncle again, but I doubt it would do any good. If I tell him Euphrastus killed a man, would it make any difference?

"Cheer up," Zobia says. "It's not the end of the world. Look, why don't we walk by Nikomedes' school? I know you like that street."

I can't tell her that it was the prospect of seeing Doros that made the street so special for me and we are unlikely to see him since it's still early in the afternoon. "We don't have to," I protest half-heartedly. "It's out of our way."

"Nonsense," she says. "Besides, I wouldn't mind spending a few minutes there again. It's a pretty spot to stop by."

So we walk to Nikomedes' school and sit for a while on the bench under the ash trees while the birds chirp and the afternoon sunshine dapples our skin. It's pleasant but the place reminds me of Doros and how far beyond my reach he is. Zobia natters on by my side, but I hardly notice what she's saying. I think of Aspasia, risking her life to care for the man she loves like a heroine in a tragedy by Aeschylus or Sophocles. If she can be so strong, why am I giving up so easily? Surely there is something I can do to change my fate.

By the time we arrive home, I have resolved to plead with my uncle one more time even if it gains me a beating. The rest of the afternoon I wait impatiently for him to return. But evening comes and suppertime with no sign of him. Darkness falls and the lamps are lit. I read until it's time to go to bed, but still he has not come home. The entire house seems to be holding its breath, waiting.

"Do you think he's all right?" I ask Zobia as we lie in the dark listening to a dog barking in the distance.

"Of course he's all right," she says. "I'm sure he'll be home soon."

But I can tell she's worried.

The next morning Lycurgus is still missing and everyone seems on edge. When I go down for breakfast, Nikomedes is arguing with Kalchas in the hall.

"We should be out looking for him," he insists. His scowl and the frustration in his voice suggest it's not the first time this morning he has said this.

"You know he wouldn't want you to miss school," Kalchas says. "He probably just decided to spend the night at a friend's house. Maybe he drank a bit too much wine."

"Or maybe he was robbed." Nikomedes glares at him. "Maybe he's lying somewhere hurt."

"Then someone will find him," Kalchas says calmly and reaches for another fig from the bowl on the hall table where the fruit has been laid out for breakfast.

"You don't care what happens to him," Nikomedes accuses.

Kalchas frowns. Maybe Nikomedes realizes he has gone too far.

"Please. I can't go to school not knowing what's happened to him."

I pick up a pomegranate and slice it open. Myrrine steps in from the courtyard and sets down a plate of dried fish she has just heated on the brazier.

"Myrrine, tell him," Nikomedes pleads. "We have to look for my father."

"We don't know that anything is wrong," she says quietly.

"He could be injured. He could be sick."

"Perhaps we should notify the watch," Myrrine suggests, looking at Kalchas.

"He'll have a fit if he's just sleeping it off somewhere," Kalchas replies, reaching for a piece of fish.

"We can't just do nothing," Nikomedes objects.

There is silence.

"All right," Kalchas says, relenting. "You can stay home, but only on one condition—you stay here. I'll go out and search for your father."

Nikomedes hesitates, as if about to argue. But evidently he thinks better of it. "All right."

I know Nikomedes will not leave it at that. He has agreed just so Kalchas will search for his father. He has no intention of staying home. But no one asks my opinion so I keep it to myself.

After breakfast Kalchas leaves to begin the search. The women retreat to the loom room and the daily chore of spinning and weaving. Of course I'm expected to help, especially now that we are short on hands. But spinning is such boring work, and I keep wondering what Nikomedes is doing. I'm certain he's going to leave the house whether he has permission or not. Finally I put down my distaff and spindle and stretch. It is only a few steps to the door, but before I can reach it Myrrine says, "Where are you going?"

They all three look at me—Zobia, Lede, and Myrrine.

"I'm just going to check on Nikomedes."

"Mind you come right back."

That is all the permission I need to feel I've been released. I fly downstairs, where I find Nikomedes near the door lacing up his knee-high sandals, preparing to leave the house, just as I suspected.

"What are you doing?" I ask.

"What does it look like?"

"You promised Kalchas you wouldn't go out."

"I didn't promise."

While this is technically true, it isn't how Kalchas would see it.

I watch his fingers deftly tying the laces. "He'll beat you if he finds out."

"I don't care." He flips that stray lock of hair out of his eyes with a toss of his head.

I know I should try to talk him out of leaving the house. He'll be in trouble if he goes. "Kalchas will find him," I say.

"Suppose he's hurt?" Nikomedes demands. "He's all I have left."

I have no answer to this. I know what it's like to lose a mother. And if my father were missing, wouldn't I go in search of him?

He reaches for his small hunting knife lying on the table next to him and tucks it under his sandal laces. It isn't much protection if he runs into trouble. I wonder what sort of trouble he might run into. Purse snatchers? Rioters? Scythians?

"Where will you go?" I ask.

He shrugs. "The Ceramicus, I suppose. That's where he goes to gamble."

"I'll go with you." I think this is a good idea as soon as I say it. I'm older than Nikomedes. I can help keep him out of trouble. And of course hunting for Lycurgus would be much more interesting than toiling in the loom room.

"It's no place for a girl," he says with a scowl. "It's not safe there."

I'm tired of being told the streets aren't safe and that I have to stay at home because I'm a girl. "I can help you look," I argue. "Besides, there's safety in numbers. Two should be safer than one."

He hesitates. I can see him turning this over in his mind. "All right, but don't say I didn't warn you."

I think secretly he's glad to have me come along, although of course he won't admit it.

I dash back to my room for my mantle. To go out

bareheaded and bare armed would attract too much attention, but I have to be quick or Nikomedes may decide to leave without me. I rush past the loom room, hoping the women won't notice. Of course they do.

"Rhea?" Myrrine calls out.

I skid back to the doorway, my mantle clutched behind my back so she won't see it. All three women look up.

"Aren't you coming back?" Myrrine asks.

"I'm helping Nikomedes," I say, which is not exactly a lie.

"What? With his lessons?"

This reason seems as good as any other and saves me from having to think of one. "Yes," I say and hold my breath. If she guesses what we are going to do, she will never let me go and she will try to stop Nikomedes too. He will be furious with me if that happens.

Myrrine looks at me suspiciously. I hold my chin a little higher and do my best to look innocent. "Well, mind you behave yourselves."

Released, I fly down the stairs before she can change her mind. I wonder how soon she or Zobia will notice that we are missing, then push that thought out of my head. No use worrying about the consequences. I told Nikomedes I would go with him, and I will. If our situations were reversed, he would do the same for me.

Nikomedes is waiting at the door, looking impatient to leave. We slip out as quietly as a pair of thieves, then set off running wildly down the street. Anyone who sees us must think we are crazy.

We don't pause for breath until we reach the statue of Hermes on the corner.

"Where to?" I say. "The Ceramicus?"

He shakes his head. "No, let's try the Painted Stoa first to see if we can find someone who might know where my father is."

"All right. The Painted Stoa it is." I'm quite willing to go anywhere he wants. It feels so good to be free with the blue sky above us and the sun beating down.

CHAPTER 19

The Painted Stoa is a favorite place for the men of the city, at least those who don't have to spend their time at a trade, to gather and discuss the latest news with their friends. News is posted there for all to read. It's a pleasant place to stroll about in the shade of the colonnade with the agora spread out before it and the much admired wall paintings of battle scenes to admire.

However, being in such a male domain makes me feel a little uncomfortable, so I let Nikomedes take the lead. After approaching several men and asking if they have seen his father, he spots one of his father's friends, a bald man of about fifty whom he recognizes. He walks up to the man and greets him while I hang back, conscious that I'm attracting stares.

"I'm looking for my father," he says. "Have you seen him?"

"Why, no, I haven't," the man answers. "It's Nikomedes,

isn't it? I saw you pouring wine at one of your father's banquets. Shouldn't you be in school?"

"Ordinarily I would be, but my mother died recently," Nikomedes says without missing a beat. It's the perfect response. You can see the little jolt of reaction in the man. I would not have thought my cousin capable of such subtle manipulation.

"That's right. So sorry to hear about that. Awful thing, this plague. I lost my youngest daughter to it not three months back."

Having distracted the man from the sticky question of why he's not at school, Nikomedes adroitly brings the conversation back to what he wants to know.

"About my father . . ." He furrows his brow. "It's important that I find him."

"Well, I'm sorry I can't help you. I haven't seen him this morning. Nothing wrong, I hope?"

Nikomedes hesitates, and fearing that he has run out of clever responses, I step forward to help him. "He's needed at home."

The man looks at me. "Who's this? Your sister?"

"My cousin. She's helping me search for my father."

The man glances about. "Are you alone?"

"No, of course not. My pedagogue is over there at the fish shop." Nikomedes points toward a row of stalls in the agora.

The man looks relieved. "Oh, well, then, that's all right. You want to be careful though. A boy your age is bound to attract attention. Your pedagogue really shouldn't let you out of his sight."

"I can take care of myself," Nikomedes says, standing straighter.

The man looks amused. He glances at me again. "Well, your cousin then. Think about her. The agora is hardly the place for a young woman. She ought to be at home at her loom."

I'm about to tell him I too can take care of myself when Nikomedes shoots me a warning look.

"Do you know anyone else who might know where my father is?" Nikomedes asks. "It's really urgent that we find him."

The man shakes his head. "Your father hasn't exactly been himself since your mother died, but you probably already know that." He looks uncomfortable. "He's been spending quite a bit of time in the Ceramicus."

"Where in the Ceramicus?" Nikomedes asks.

The man looks as if he doesn't want to answer this question, but after a brief inner struggle, he says, "The House of the Egyptian. But you shouldn't go there yourself, and certainly not with your cousin. Send one of your slaves to see if he's there."

"Thank you for your advice," Nikomedes says politely. "We'll do that. And now we'd better go find my pedagogue. If you'll excuse us . . . ?"

"Of course."

I wait until we are out of earshot. "You do know we'll be in a lot of trouble if we go there," I tell Nikomedes in a low voice as we walk away from the Painted Stoa. "You know what that place is, don't you?"

"Of course I do. It's a brothel."

I glance around quickly to see if anyone has overheard. I don't think they have.

"We could tell Kalchas," I suggest, knowing there is little chance Nikomedes will agree to this.

He frowns. "Go back if you want. I'm going to find my father." His jaw has that set look he gets when his mind is made up.

I sigh. "Of course I'm not going back. Someone's got to make sure you don't get into trouble." This is true, but I also feel excited at the prospect of another chance to explore the Ceramicus. I would far rather wander about the Ceramicus any day than sort wool or spin.

We cut through the agora, which is crowded enough that no one pays attention to us. Tradesmen cry out their wares, and so do the women selling figs, the fruit vendors, the butchers, and the flower girls. Soon enough we have made our way through all the noise and bustle and emerged in the broad thoroughfare of the Panathenaic Way, the route taken by the sacred processions from the Dipylon Gate to the Acropolis. There are people here too but it's not as noisy as the agora.

"So you know where it is?" I ask as we face the crowded mud-brick buildings that make up the Ceramicus, the section of the city where the potters, leather-workers, and other craftsmen live and have their workshops. It seems to me that we might wander a long time in that maze of narrow streets without stumbling upon the House of the Egyptian.

Nikomedes avoids my eyes.

"We could ask someone," I suggest, noticing a burly

tradesman coming toward us. But when he reaches us, I don't have the nerve to ask for directions to a brothel, and neither does Nikomedes. The man passes by with barely a glance at us. So we walk on, still with no idea how to find the place.

Two more men pass us who look at us curiously. I'm sure they can tell that we don't belong here. It isn't just that we're young and unchaperoned; our clothes give us away too. We don't wear the rough garb of tradesmen or manual workers. I just hope we don't run into anyone who might try to rob us. Do we look like easy prey? I try to push that thought out of my mind.

Eventually we come to a fork in the street and have to choose which way to go. Nikomedes favors the street that forks to the right, and since they both look similar, I don't argue. This street leads to an even narrower street where we see a pottery sign in front of the first house we come to and a silversmith sign in front of the next. I'm about to suggest again that we ask for directions when I hear a flute and a lyre. It sounds familiar and then I realize it's very much like the tune Chloe was playing that day I was wandering about the Ceramicus so distracted.

"Do you hear that?" I ask.

"You mean the flute?" Nikomedes squints up at the narrow windows of the house across from us. "What about it?"

"I've heard that before."

"So?"

I know I might be mistaken. What are the chances that it could be Chloe? This is not the area of the Ceramicus where

Aspasia lives. Then I remember that Aspasia said she sent Chloe and Nessa away to a place where they would be safe from the plague. Maybe this is where she sent them.

"What is it?" Nikomedes asks.

"I'm going over there and knock," I say, suddenly making up my mind. "It can't hurt to ask for directions."

"No, wait—"

Before he can stop me, I cross the narrow street, walk up to the house, and knock on the door. Nikomedes waves frantically for me to come away while there is still time, but I ignore him. When the door opens, before me stands Chloe holding her flute with Nessa peeking out behind her, a lyre in her hands.

"Rhea!" Chloe exclaims. "What are you doing here? Did Aspasia send you?"

She catches sight of Nikomedes, who is standing stock-still in the street staring at us. "Who's your friend?" She lowers her voice. "Is he your boyfriend?"

I feel the blood rush to my cheeks. "My cousin."

"Oh. He's cute." She waves at him, and Nikomedes ducks his head, embarrassed.

I can only hope he won't mention this later. My uncle has no idea I know acrobats and flute girls, and I'm sure he wouldn't approve.

"Did you come to visit me?" Chloe asks.

"I heard your flute."

"You were just passing by?" She glances curiously at Nikomedes.

"We're looking for the House of the Egyptian," I tell her. "It's supposed to be somewhere around here."

She looks surprised. "The House of the Egyptian? Whatever for?"

"We think Nikomedes' father is there. He didn't come home last night and we're worried about him. Do you know where it is?"

She glances at Nikomedes again. "I do. In fact, I can take you there. But do you know what it is? It's not the sort of place—"

"We know. It's a brothel."

She takes a deep breath. "All right then. If you're sure about this."

"We are," I assure her.

She gives Nessa a push and disappears inside, returning a minute later with a sea-green mantle draped over her light brown hair and covering her arms. "My music teacher is a bit of a grouch, but I assured her Aspasia would have let me show my dear friend to her relative's house, so she let me go. Nessa wanted to come too, but I told her she couldn't. She'll pout for a while, but I'll let her wear my silver comb later and all will be well."

I introduce her to Nikomedes, who scowls and says almost nothing but then steals glances at her when he thinks she isn't looking. At first I think he's shocked because she's a flute girl, but as we continue up the street, I decide he's just shy. After all, except for me, he isn't used to being around girls.

Meanwhile, Chloe doesn't seem to notice and chatters away as she leads us up one winding street after another. Just as I begin to feel hopelessly lost, we come to a house with an enigmatic sign painted on the front—an eye inside

of a triangle. I know what it means. It's the eye of Re, the
Egyptian sun god.

CHAPTER 20

Whe stand there a moment staring at the house, which is no different from all the other houses on the street, the same sunbaked mud-brick walls and orange barrel-tiled roof. Now that we have actually found the House of the Egyptian, I question the wisdom of coming here. I can imagine the scolding Zobia will give me when she finds out. And that might be nothing compared to my uncle's anger. But then I remind myself why we are here — to find my uncle if we can. As Nikomedes said, he could be lying somewhere sick with plague and dying. Or maybe he has been beaten and robbed. The answer to his whereabouts may be behind that door.

"I suppose we should knock," Chloe says, breaking the silence. Even she seems uncertain.

Perhaps that's all it takes to make Nikomedes feel bold. He steps forward looking determined and raps with the brass knocker shaped like a coiled snake. We stand there another minute or two before the door is opened by a sultry woman in a long saffron tunic. Her dark eyes are lined with kohl, her cheeks rouged, and her lips painted bloodred. She looks us over disdainfully.

"What do you want?" she asks in a foreign accent.

"I'm looking for my father, Lycurgus, son of Hippias," Nikomedes announces as if he were the head of the Scythian guard looking for a thief. I had no idea he could sound so official. My opinion of Nikomedes goes up a notch.

"He's not here. Go away." She starts to shut the door in his face.

Nikomedes places his foot on the threshold to keep the door from closing. "May we come in and look?"

The woman smiles contemptuously. "Little boy, come back when you have hair on your chin."

But Nikomedes is not put off so easily.

"If you refuse to let us in, we'll tell the magistrate you're hiding runaway slaves," he warns. I can't believe his audacity.

The woman looks at Chloe and me, then back to Nikomedes. "That's a very big threat from one so young."

"Maia," a man's voice calls from within. "What's going on?"

"A boy," she throws back over her shoulder in heavily accented Greek. "He says his father is here. He wants to come in to look for him. He threatens to tell the magistrate we have runaway slaves here if we don't let him in."

"Oh, for god's sake, then let him in," the man says impatiently. "I don't want the magistrate nosing about."

She shrugs and steps aside to let us enter. Nikomedes

goes first, with Chloe and me close on his heels. The woman surveys us with calculating eyes. Instinctively I move closer to Chloe. I don't feel nearly as brave now as I felt at the Painted Stoa.

"Who are you looking for, boy?" the man asks. He ignores Chloe and me.

We can see him now, an older man with a neatly trimmed black beard and a hawk-like nose seated at a table with scrolls spread out around him. He is darker than most Greeks and has large, rather prominent eyes. Probably, like the woman, he is a foreigner.

"Lycurgus, son of Hippias," Nikomedes repeats.

"You aren't just saying that to get in here, are you?" the man asks suspiciously. "How old are you anyway?"

"Fifteen," Nikomedes responds.

Of course I know he's only thirteen but I don't say anything. This is no time to quibble. If he can bluff his way in, great.

"Well, show the boy about," the man snaps at the woman with a dismissive wave of his hand. "We have nothing to hide."

She seems reluctant but then shrugs again and motions with a crook of her finger for us to follow her. With a look of boredom and disdain on her face, she leads us through a maze of rooms with murals painted on the walls depicting gods in amorous pursuit of mortals—Zeus as an eagle swooping down on Ganymede, Zeus as a bull bearing away Europa on his back, Apollo pursuing Daphne, Hades abducting Persephone. The doorways are hung with colored beads and the air is heavy with perfumes. A dusky bare-breasted woman comes to her door and stares at us with cat eyes. Her hair is coal-black, gold bangles encircle her arms, and her nipples are painted black. I have never seen anyone like her before, and I think if it were not for Nikomedes and Chloe, I might turn and run.

"Have you seen enough?" our guide asks with an arched eyebrow, looking at each of us in turn.

"I was told my father is here," Nikomedes says stubbornly.

"Well, then you were told wrong."

"What's in that room?" Chloe asks, plucking up her courage and pointing at the last doorway.

The woman shrugs. "See for yourself."

I'm afraid of what we will see, but I stay close to Nikomedes and Chloe, not wanting to be left alone with the two strange women. In the last room a sleeping man sprawls facedown on a bed, his hand trailing on the floor beside an overturned cup. This can't be my uncle. Disappointed, I turn away, but Nikomedes parts the bead curtain and steps into the room. He hesitates, then leans over the man and touches his arm.

"Father?"

"Is it him?" Chloe whispers in my ear.

I'm not sure. We follow Nikomedes into the room. There is a mural on the wall here too, a scantily-clad Aphrodite rising from the sea foam and a naked Eros with his quiver of arrows. Nikomedes shakes the man's shoulder, trying to wake him. The man stirs and turns toward us. With a shock I recognize my uncle, but I have never seen him looking like this before—chest bare, bleary-eyed, unkempt, dissolute. He might be one of the refugees who beg for alms in the streets. I avert my eyes to avoid embarrassing him. He would not want me to see him like this.

"Father," Nikomedes says, "we've been searching for you. Are you all right?"

Lycurgus raises himself enough to frown at Nikomedes. "Where am I?"

"The House of the Egyptian."

He rubs the back of his arm across his eyes and blinks. "What are you doing here?"

"We came to find you. You didn't come home last night, and we were worried."

"You shouldn't be here."

"Can you stand?" Nikomedes asks.

"Where's Kalchas?"

"He isn't here. It's just me — and Rhea — and . . ." His eyes flick to Chloe, then away.

"Rhea?" My uncle's eyes fly to me. "What's she doing here? You brought your cousin to a place like this? What were you thinking?"

"She helped me find you."

"Why isn't she at home where she belongs?" He sounds angry.

"Please come home with us." Nikomedes' voice almost breaks.

With effort Lycurgus sits up. He buries his head in his hands. "What time is it?"

"Midday."

"Why aren't you in school?"

Nikomedes doesn't answer. He glances at the painting of Aphrodite on the wall, then quickly looks away again.

"Where the bloody hell is Kalchas?" demands his father.

"He's out looking for you."

"He let you and your cousin go out alone? I'll have him flogged."

"He doesn't know. It isn't his fault. Now let's go home. Please, Father."

Lycurgus staggers to his feet and tugs his tunic over his left shoulder. Leaning on Nikomedes, he stumbles toward the door. I'm not sure he has noticed Chloe and she shrinks back, apparently not eager to be noticed. Haltingly we retrace our steps through the maze of rooms past erotic murals, beaded doorways, and half glimpsed women. In the outermost room the man with the prominent eyes and the hawk-like nose watches us leave without a word.

Once outside, Lycurgus steadies himself with a hand on Nikomedes' shoulder and blinks at the bright sunlight. When he has his bearings, they start walking. Chloe and I follow at a little distance.

"Your uncle is lucky you found him when you did," she says in a low voice. "The House of the Egyptian has a bad reputation. Men have disappeared there."

"He wasn't like this until my aunt died from the plague," I tell her, not wanting her to judge him too harshly.

She gives my hand a sympathetic squeeze. "Any luck at getting out of the marriage to Euphrastus?"

I shake my head. "Unfortunately, no."

"Aspasia couldn't help you?"

"She has her own worries now."

Chloe sighs. "I guess so. What will you do now?"

"I don't know. My uncle has moved up the day of the wedding. It's only ten days away now."

"Can't you try to talk to him again?"

I look at Lycurgus's back as he plods along, leaning on Nikomedes. I'm glad for Nikomedes' sake that we found him, but I doubt it will change his plans for me. There is still that gambling debt to be repaid.

"I heard Euphrastus killed a man," I tell her.

"It wouldn't surprise me," she says. "Anyone can see he's dangerous. Have you told your uncle?"

I shake my head. "I'm not sure it would make any difference. He's so determined for this marriage to take place."

"We could still paint you blue," she murmurs.

I smile half-heartedly. If only it were as simple as that.

Nikomedes turns his head every so often to look back at us, but Lycurgus never glances back. No doubt he would prefer that we had not witnessed his shame. I wonder if he remembers Chloe from the banquet. So far he has given no indication that he recognizes her. In fact, she might as well be invisible. When we come to the street where she and Nessa are staying with their music teacher, she squeezes my hand again before slipping away.

CHAPTER 21

When we finally arrive home, the women come running. They fuss over Lycurgus as if he has returned from the dead, ignoring Nikomedes and me until he has been bathed and put to bed.

Then Zobia brings water up to the women's quarters for my bath and gives me a good scolding.

"How could you run off like that?" she demands as I step into the basin. "You know you shouldn't go out alone."

"I wasn't alone," I object as she pours cool water over me. "I was with Nikomedes."

"That doesn't make it okay. What were you thinking, taking off without a word to anyone?"

"I knew you and Myrrine would say no." I tilt my head back and close my eyes, letting the water flow over my face. It feels good to let the dust wash away.

"Of course we'd say no. And for a very good reason. You should not be running about the streets like a fisherman's daughter."

She goes on like that as she scrubs my back. I just keep quiet and let her rant. She will hear about the House of the Egyptian sooner or later, and then there will be another scolding. No reason to spring the full extent of my infractions on her all at once.

Gradually the household calms down. After my bath, I retreat to the loom room, feeling fresh and clean, and dutifully spin wool while Lede sorts and Zobia weaves. That's where Myrrine finds me an hour later.

"Your uncle wants to see you downstairs," she says grimly. I can tell by her tone that I'm in trouble.

Zobia and Lede exchange quick glances.

"What does he want?" I ask warily.

"I don't know, but you'd better not keep him waiting," Myrrine says.

"I'm glad I'm not in your shoes," Lede tells me.

I have a sick feeling in the pit of my stomach as I lay down my spindle.

"Be brave," Zobia says.

"Wait." Myrrine stops me in the doorway and tucks a lock of hair behind my ear. "There. That's better." She smiles but I can tell she's worried.

I follow her down the stairs, my throat constricted. At the door of my uncle's study, she leaves me. I would like to turn and rush out of the house. Knowing what a temper my uncle has, I dread what he is going to say.

He's pacing. I can tell by his scowl that he's in a bad mood. I try to look contrite as I wait for him to notice me. When he does, he motions impatiently for me to enter.

He paces back and forth several more times before he

begins. "I know you were not the one to make the decision to leave the house today. Nikomedes has confessed that it was his idea." This is true, but I can't let Nikomedes take all the blame. Before I can speak, he rushes on. "I understand that you both were worried about my welfare. Nevertheless, neither of you should have left the house without supervision. You both should have known better. Nikomedes deliberately disobeyed Kalchas and he has been punished for it."

That's when I notice the cane in his hand and feel a sinking in the pit of my stomach. Has he given Nikomedes a beating? He gives me no chance to ask, and I sense that to interrupt him might make the situation worse. At least he isn't shouting. His anger seems to be under control.

"As your guardian, Rhea, I'm responsible for your behavior as well. I have tried to be patient with you out of consideration for your feelings of grief at the loss of your family. However, you have repeatedly defied me. When a man has a horse which fails to obey his commands, he has to break it. The same is true of disobedient children. I would be lax in my duty not to treat you as if you were my own daughter."

I can't take my eyes off the cane. I have never had a beating in my life. Is he really going to beat me?

"I realize my dear brother did not discipline you as he should have. He was tender-hearted and indulgent to both you and your brother. I fear in your case it was not a kindness and did not prepare you for a woman's lot."

I stand very still and try to slow the pounding of my heart. I must not show him I'm afraid. No matter what happens, I must be strong. I owe it to my parents. I am their daughter. I will not shame them.

"If you prefer to have servants come to hold you, I will call them."

The idea of being held down by servants while my uncle beats me is humiliating. I shake my head, not trusting myself to speak. If Nikomedes could bear it, so can I. I turn my back to him and close my eyes, tensing for the first blow. How many of them will there be? How bad will it hurt? I clench my teeth, determined not to cry out. I won't give him the satisfaction.

When the first blow comes, I gasp but stand my ground. Then the second comes and the third. They hurt worse than anything I have ever felt. There are six in all, delivered one after another. My eyes fill with tears, but I blink them back, unwilling to let my uncle see me cry. He has beat me like a common slave. I hate him and vow to run away. I won't stay under the roof of a man who has treated me so cruelly.

"I hope this has been a lesson, and that in the future you will behave in a more modest and womanly way," he says when he is done, not looking at me. "I have done this for your own good. A respectable young woman should never set foot in an establishment of the sort you did today. You are old enough to know better. When you are a married woman, your husband will expect you to behave in a manner that won't tarnish his reputation. If you don't, he may punish you far worse than I have. Let it be a lesson."

I just stand there with my back to him, hating him with every fiber of my being.

"Go on," he says. "We're done here. I hope you don't give me cause to do this again."

I run upstairs, fling myself on my bed, and let all my pent-up emotion pour out. I sob and cry and pound my pillow. Soon Zobia is there, trying to comfort me.

"Rhea," she croons, taking me into her arms.

"He beat me," I choke out, still roiling with emotion.

"There, there." She strokes my hair. "It's over now. Let it go."

"I hate him!" I say with vehemence.

"No, you don't. He's your uncle and he means well. His whole world has fallen apart. He doesn't know what to do."

"I won't stay here. I won't!"

"You have no place else to go. And soon enough you'll be a married woman living in your husband's house."

"I won't marry Euphrastus!"

"You have no choice." Her voice is calm, soothing. "You must marry the man your uncle chooses. If you refuse, he can sell you into slavery. It may seem cruel, but that's the law."

"I'd rather die!"

"Don't say such a terrible thing. You don't mean it. What would your poor mother and father think? Would you be so quick to throw away the life the gods have given you?"

She rocks me in her arms just as she did when I was a child.

"I miss them so much," I say, still crying, but with the anger ebbing now.

"I know you do."

"You won't leave me, will you, Zobia?"

"No, of course not. What a question! Now dry your tears and get ready for supper."

"I don't want to go down. I don't want to ever see him again."

"Do you think Nikomedes will stay in his room and pout?"

I forgot about Nikomedes. No, I don't think he'll stay in his room and pout. He'll be at supper as if nothing happened. Zobia is right. I can't stay up here. If I do, my uncle will have won. I must show him he hasn't won.

CHAPTER 22

It turns out I don't have to worry about seeing my uncle when I go downstairs for supper. He's retired early. Nikomedes and Kalchas join the women in the courtyard, eating around the brazier. No one says anything about the punishment Lycurgus has inflicted on Nikomedes or me. We both eat in silence, avoiding each other's eyes. My uncle may think I'm more resigned to my rapidly approaching marriage after the beating, but in truth I'm as determined as ever to avoid it, even if it means being sold into slavery. As I eat, a plan begins to form in my mind. By the end of the meal I know what I must do. If I can't persuade my uncle to change his mind, then I must try to persuade Euphrastus to change his. I don't know why I didn't think of this before. Now I just have to find out where he lives and pay him a visit. Surely someone can tell me where he lives.

A little later when Zobia is sitting with old Xantippe and no one else is watching, I slip downstairs. Nikomedes is in the dining room, memorizing lines from Homer by the light of an oil lamp. As luck would have it, Kalchas has stepped out of the room, giving me a chance to speak to Nikomedes alone.

He looks up startled when I enter the room. "What are you doing down here?"

"Where's Kalchas?" I ask.

"Outside I guess. Why? Do you want to talk to him?"

"No, I want to talk to you."

He frowns. "Me? Why do you want to talk to me?"

"Do you know where Euphrastus lives?"

He shakes his head. "Why would I know that?"

"I thought you might." I bite my lip, disappointed. But then I knew it was a long shot.

"Why do you want to know?" he asks, curious now.

I glance at the doorway, knowing Kalchas may return at any moment. "I want to talk to him."

"Why?"

"Maybe I could change his mind."

Nikomedes considers this. "You mean about marrying you? How?"

I glance at the door again. "I could tell him what a bad wife I'd make."

Nikomedes snorts. "You think he'd care?"

"I have to try." Surely he sees that? I can't just give up. If Euphrastus knew what a poor wife I'd make, why would he want to marry me?

"I could ask my father where he lives," Nikomedes suggests.

"No."

"So how are you going to find him?"

I hesitate. "I could ask Chloe. She might know."

He stares at the tablet in front of him and fiddles with his stylus. Maybe he disapproves of my friendship with Chloe. I'm about to tell him to forget I asked when he says, "You mean, go to the Ceramicus again?"

I don't blame him for being wary since our trip there earlier in the day cost us both a beating.

"It's the only way I know to get hold of her."

"Do you want me to go with you? You probably shouldn't go alone. You ought to have someone with you."

I roll my eyes. "I can take Zobia."

"She's just an old woman," he says dismissively. As if he would be so much more protection.

"I didn't think you'd want to go after—"

"Do you think she has a boyfriend?" he interrupts.

I blink. Of course he means Chloe, not Zobia, but why would he ask such a question? Why does he care if Chloe has a boyfriend?

"I think there's someone she likes," I concede.

He looks disappointed, or is that just my imagination? Surely he doesn't have a crush on her. She's a flute girl. His father would have a stroke if he got friendly with a flute girl. That might be an even worse offense than visiting the House of the Egyptian.

"Perhaps it would be better if you didn't go," I suggest, foreseeing problems.

"Go where?" Kalchas asks in his deep voice from the doorway.

We both start guiltily. How long has he been standing

there? We probably look like a pair of thieves planning to steal a god from a shrine.

"To the Acropolis," I say, thinking fast. You have to be fast to outwit Kalchas.

"And why shouldn't he go to the Acropolis?" Kalchas asks quietly, watching me. It's as if he can see inside my head. I look away nervously.

"No reason at all," Nikomedes says.

Kalchas frowns at us. "I don't know what you two are plotting, but get it out of your heads right now. Wasn't a beating enough to teach you both a lesson? Are you so eager for another?" He steps into the room. "Now off with you," he tells me. "I'll help the boy with his schoolwork. You've caused enough trouble for one day."

Me? He thinks I'm responsible for our visit to the House of the Egyptian? That is so unfair. But I sense arguing will do no good. I leave, but later when I go down to fetch a cup of water for old Xantippe, Nikomedes hears me and intercepts me as I'm about to go back up.

"If you go to see your friend Chloe, I want to go with you," he says in a low determined voice as I stand with one foot on the first step of the stairs. "And if you go to see Euphrastus, I want to go there too. It's too dangerous for you to go alone or with Zobia."

I don't think it's too dangerous, but I prefer not to go alone. Especially to see Euphrastus. I'd like some backup when that meeting takes place. I have no idea how cordial he'll be if I show up at his door asking to be released from the marriage arrangement.

"What about Kalchas?" I say, glancing at the door to the

dining room and keeping my voice low too. "You know he won't let you out of his sight."

"I'll think of something," he promises.

There isn't time to argue, so I agree and continue up the stairs.

I take old Xantippe her cup of water, nod when she calls me Nysa, listen to her ramble on about a party she attended in the distant past, then retire to my room. I'm just unfurling a scroll of Sappho's poems, hoping to read a little before bedtime, when Myrrine walks in. She sits down on the bed beside me and smoothes a wrinkle from my blanket.

"I'm sorry you got a beating today," she says, "but you know you shouldn't run off like that."

"What did we do that was so wrong?" I ask. "We went in search of my uncle when we didn't know if he was ill with plague or had been beaten and robbed. We found him and brought him home. Was that so terrible? Nikomedes would have gone alone if I hadn't gone with him."

She sighs. "Kalchas thinks you and Nikomedes are planning to leave the house again. Is that true?"

I suspect Kalchas has sent her to find out. Well, I may have endured a beating, but that has not made me more docile. "Why don't you ask Nikomedes?" I suggest.

Her forehead knits with concern. "Please, Rhea. Don't do anything that might get Kalchas in trouble. Don't you realize that if Nikomedes keeps running off, Kalchas also gets blamed? Your uncle has threatened to send him to the silver mines." Her worry is obvious, but is it my fault if my uncle threatens Kalchas?

"So I'm to stay here like a calf being fatted for sacrifice?"

She lays a hand on my arm. "This isn't just about you. Other people's lives are at stake. I know you're unhappy about your approaching marriage, but there's nothing you can do about it."

I'm tired of hearing that I can't do anything about it. They all want me to quit fighting and accept my fate. But I'm not going to.

"Do you know where he lives?" I ask.

"Who?"

"Euphrastus."

She stares at me. Then her eyes narrow with suspicion. "Why do you want to know?"

I sigh.

"No, I don't know. You aren't planning to go there, are you? Rhea, you can't. You mustn't. Tell me that's not what you're planning."

"I can't very well go there when I don't know where he lives," I grumble.

She stands up, agitated. "Put this mad idea right out of your head. Your uncle would be furious if he knew."

"Will you tell him?"

She hesitates. "No, I won't tell him."

"I can't marry Euphrastus."

"Don't you think lots of young women have thought that about the husbands their parents have chosen, but the day comes and they do because they have to, and you know what? Life doesn't come to a stop. It goes on."

I don't care about all the other young women who have given in to the demands of their parents or guardians. And who knows if their lives go on? What toll does their surrender take? Perhaps they are like the shades of the underworld, mere shadows of their former selves. And does anyone care?

"If I could just talk to him, maybe I could make him see," I explain, hoping she will understand.

"See what? What is it that you want him to see?"

"That I would never be happy with him. That I would make a terrible wife. That I'm not good at weaving or cooking or managing a household or any of those things wives are supposed to do."

"You'll learn."

"I don't want to learn."

"Rhea." She sits down again and puts an arm around me. I flinch. She has touched my back where the cane struck.

"I'm sorry. Does it hurt?"

Of course it hurts.

"May I see?"

I remove the clasp on the right shoulder of my tunic and let the back fall.

"It's not so bad. You have red welts, and they'll turn to bruises. Would you like me to put a plaster on it to ease the pain?"

I shake my head. I doubt a plaster will ease the pain. It goes too deep. Better to ache and remember the injustice of the punishment my uncle meted out. "Have you ever been beaten?"

"Yes, but never by your uncle. I give him no cause. You would be wise to do the same."

"Is it so terrible to be a slave?" I ask, wondering if I could endure it.

She pushes a stray lock of hair back from my cheek. "I hope you never have to find out."

CHAPTER 23

The next morning I know something is wrong as soon as I go downstairs. Lede rushes by me with a grim expression and not so much as a good morning. Lycurgus is shouting at Kalchas in his study and when Kalchas emerges he's glowering. Wondering what it's all about, I head for the kitchen and find Zobia preparing old Xantippe's breakfast — a piece of dried fish, a chunk of bread, and a cup of watered wine to dip the bread in.

"Why is everyone in such a bad mood?" I ask her.

She sighs. "They're worried, that's all. Nikomedes is sick. A physician's been sent for."

I stare at her. He was fine yesterday. Could he have contracted the plague while we were running about the city searching for his father?

"It's not serious, is it?" I ask uneasily.

"That's up to the physician, isn't it?"

"You think it's the plague?"

"Now don't go getting yourself upset. All I know is he was all right last night but today he's got a fever and says he aches all over, and he keeps calling out for water."

I wince. All early symptoms of the plague. "Can I see him?"

"Most certainly not. No one but Lede's to go near him. If it is the plague, we don't want everyone else catching it."

In the hall I see Lede making an offering at the altar of the household gods. A sudden cry from Nikomedes sends her scurrying to his room. I feel guilty as I slice into a pomegranate I picked up from the bowl of fruit on the hall table. It doesn't seem right that I should be eating breakfast as usual while Nikomedes may be lying ill with the plague.

When the physician comes, I seat myself on the lower steps of the stairs and try to look inconspicuous. From my vantage point I can hear the low murmur of his voice but not his words as he speaks to Lede and Nikomedes through the open door. Lycurgus paces impatiently in the hall. Although he must see me, he ignores me.

"Well, is it the plague?" he demands when the physician emerges.

The physician strokes his beard thoughtfully. "I can't be sure, but to be safe keep him isolated for now. Give him water when he's thirsty."

After the physician is gone, Lycurgus calls us all downstairs. We stand around in a cluster, exchanging nervous looks.

"I want you to make Nikomedes comfortable and see to his wants, but remember—only Lede goes into that room. Is that understood?" He gives us all a stern look, especially me.

"Now I have business to attend to at the Pnyx. I trust you all know what to do."

He is hardly out the door when Nikomedes cries out for water. Lede runs to get it for him. Before she can return with it, he cries out again, this time for his tablet.

"I'll search his schoolbag," Myrrine tells Lede as she hurries back from the kitchen with a cup of water.

I watch as Myrrine empties the contents of his schoolbag on the bench in the hall. But even after she has dumped everything out, there's no sign of his tablet.

For a while Nikomedes alternates between calling for water and crying out for his tablet. Why he's so obsessed with his tablet is a mystery to us all. Unfortunately it's nowhere to be found.

"Maybe he left it at school," Myrrine suggests to Kalchas, who has been helping to search the house for it. "Maybe you should go there and check so he doesn't wear himself out crying for it."

Kalchas utters an oath. "Why does he need his fool tablet?"

As if in response Nikomedes' cries grow louder.

"He'll make himself sicker fussing like that," Myrrine says.

"Are you sure it isn't here?" Kalchas asks in exasperation.

"We've looked everywhere."

"Blasted nuisance," he mutters.

He's clearly not happy about having to walk to Nikomedes' school in search of the tablet. The walk there and back will take at least an hour. But after more grumbling, he sets off.

As soon as he's out the door, Nikomedes calms down, as if sensing he will soon have his tablet. Relieved, we go about our daily chores, whispering when we are near his room so we won't disturb him. I feel terrible for Nikomedes, but I'm still determined to pay a visit to Chloe to ask if she knows where Euphrastus lives. Now that Kalchas is out of the house it seems the perfect time to go. But Zobia, who has a sixth sense for when I'm plotting anything, catches me in the act of taking my mantle from my chest.

"What sort of mischief are you up to?" she asks suspiciously, standing in the doorway, hands on hips.

She has caught me red-handed and I have no choice but to tell her the truth. "Please, I have to go out."

"Whatever for? You were out yesterday, and I would think the beating you got for it would be enough to make you think twice about going out again."

"I don't care. I have to see Chloe. It's really important."

"The flute girl? And if your uncle finds out?"

"Well, then I suppose he'll beat me again."

"Such a willful child. Is there nothing I can say to change your mind?"

I shake my head. "No, there isn't. I have to find out where Euphrastus lives and I don't know who else to ask."

She sighs. "Why do you have to find out where he lives? What difference does it make?"

"I have to try to talk him out of this marriage."

She looks at me with pity.

"*Please,*" I say again.

"Well, I'm not going to let you go out alone. I'm coming with you."

"What about Myrrine?"

"I'll tell her we're going to the marketplace to buy more figs. You know how Nikomedes loves figs."

I jump up and hug her. I should have known she would help me if I asked.

When Zobia tells Myrrine our plan to go to the agora for figs, Myrrine agrees distractedly. "It may help. Poor thing, he seems to be suffering."

I feel guilty sneaking off when Nikomedes is sick, and probably Zobia does too. But there is no time to lose. We must take advantage of Kalchas' absence. If we aren't back before he returns, he will question what we are up to. We can't take the chance that he will keep our secret.

We are barely out of sight of the house when Nikomedes comes loping after us. Zobia cries out when she sees him and claps a hand to her mouth. I take a step back and stare at him. Why is he out of bed?

"It's all right," he says. "I don't have the plague. See." He flaps his arms and hops about in a most alarming manner for someone who's supposed to be sick. I glance about, hoping none of the neighbors notice. They will surely think he's lost his mind.

"But your fever!" Zobia protests.

He grins. "I stood on my head. And I rubbed my eyes to make them red."

"You're not sick?"

"I was only pretending to be sick to get rid of Kalchas." He seems quite proud of himself.

"What a mean trick," she says. "You should be ashamed of yourself. Wait till Kalchas hears about this."

"How else was I supposed to get rid of him?" Nikomedes demands. "And if you tell him, I'll tell my father you and Rhea sneaked off to see her friend in the Ceramicus."

"We're only off to market to get some figs for you," she insists. "I thought you were sick. I should have known it was one of your pranks. You should be ashamed of yourself for making everyone worry."

He crosses his arms over his chest and looks stubborn. "I know you're going to the Ceramicus to see Rhea's friend."

Zobia gives me a reproachful look.

"I asked him for help, but I didn't know he would fake an illness," I tell her.

"So if you want your secret kept, you'll just have to take me along," he concludes cheerfully.

There is no way Zobia can force him to go back to the house, and she knows it. She sighs deeply.

"Well, Kalchas will be back soon enough and when he finds out you're not sick in your bed, you'll get another beating," she warns.

"If we go fast enough, we'll be back before he is," Nikomedes points out.

"And what if Lede goes in and finds you missing?"

"She won't. I rolled a blanket to make it look like I'm lying there. She'll be so glad I'm sleeping that I doubt she'll try to wake me."

I have to admit Nikomedes seems to have thought of everything. I never dreamed he was capable of being so sneaky.

"And what will your father say when he finds out you were only pretending to be sick?" Zobia asks.

"I don't intend for him to find out. I'll just get better. He'll be so relieved I don't have the plague, he won't question it."

"Oh, won't he?"

But I think she sees she has lost the argument.

"Not unless you give me away."

She sighs again and looks at me. "I suppose you two had this all planned?"

"No, I didn't know he would . . ." I stop, feeling guilty. Nikomedes had said he would figure out a way to give Kalchas the slip and he had. "He really wanted to come along," I finish lamely.

"And why was that?"

I glance at Nikomedes, but he avoids my eyes.

"He's trying to help me."

"You shouldn't encourage him. Bad enough that you get yourself into trouble. You shouldn't get your cousin in trouble too."

I could argue that I tried to talk him out of it, but I suppose I didn't try very hard. And if we get into trouble, Zobia will get blamed too. We will just have to get back before anyone discovers what we are up to. That means we have no time to waste. We set off and are soon navigating the maze of narrow streets in the Ceramicus. After making a few wrong turns, we locate the street where Chloe is staying with her music teacher. This time I recognize the house, although it looks identical to the houses around it, all equally blank-faced and sun-bleached.

Nessa answers our knock and looks with big dark eyes at each of us. Then she turns and shouts for Chloe. You wouldn't think such a small person could shout so loudly. She would make an excellent commander leading her troops into battle.

A moment later Chloe appears, a little breathless, as if she ran to answer the summons. She's wearing an ankle-length pink tunic and has a pink ribbon braided in her hair. She hugs me and then flashes a smile at Nikomedes, who is again staring at her as if he has never seen a girl before. By now I'm pretty sure she's the reason he was so keen on coming.

"I'm sorry I can't invite you in," she says, looking over her shoulder. "My music teacher is terribly strict."

"It doesn't matter," I assure her. "We have to get back before anyone notices Nikomedes is gone and he gets into trouble."

She glances at Nikomedes, who immediately looks at his feet. "Why will you get into trouble?"

"He's supposed to be sick in bed," I answer for him. "It's a long story and we don't have much time. I'm trying to find out where Euphrastus lives. I thought maybe you would know."

"Sorry. No."

"Do you think Aspasia would know?"

She lays her hand on my arm. "You can't go there, Rhea. It's too dangerous. You could catch the plague."

"I could catch the plague walking through the streets of Athens."

"It's not the same as walking into a home where the plague has struck," she says solemnly.

"At last some sense," Zobia murmurs behind me.

"Why are you trying to find out where he lives?" Chloe asks.

"I want to ask him to release me from the marriage arrangement."

"You won't go see him alone, will you?" Her forehead crinkles with worry.

"I'll go with her," Nikomedes says, standing a little straighter, no longer looking at his feet.

"You most certainly will not," Zobia snaps. "Bad enough that you pretended to have the plague today. You can't pull that trick twice."

"You pretended to have the plague?" Chloe says, amused.

Nikomedes reddens and shifts awkwardly from one foot to the other.

From within we hear a woman's voice call Chloe's name.

"That's my music teacher," she says, grimacing. "I'd better go. I have a new tune to practice for a banquet tonight. I told her the guests will probably be too drunk to know if I'm playing the right notes or not, but she insists I get it perfect. Sorry I can't help you."

When the door closes, Nikomedes looks as disappointed as I am. He stares at the door as if hoping it will open again.

"What do we do now?" he asks.

"We go back home and hope that we get there before Kalchas does," Zobia says briskly. "Otherwise we're all going to be in a lot of trouble."

CHAPTER 24

My heart is heavy as we retrace our steps through the narrow winding streets. I don't feel like talking and evidently neither do my companions. Zobia keeps pausing to catch her breath, and this slows us down. I don't think we'll get home before Kalchas, and I wonder glumly how he will punish Nikomedes for having feigned his illness and how we'll all be punished for leaving the house. Just as I am feeling truly discouraged, I notice a familiar figure emerge from one of the houses ahead of us. With a small jolt of surprise I recognize Maron. He starts off at a brisk pace without glancing in our direction. It's the first time I've seen him since that night I ran into him at the amphitheater. The sight of him reminds me of the kiss and the awkwardness it caused between us.

"Isn't that your sculptor?" Zobia says, squinting.

"I don't think so," I say.

"What sculptor?" Nikomedes asks, waking from the daze he has been in since Chloe closed the door.

"I wonder what he's doing here," Zobia says thoughtfully.

"Maybe it's just someone who looks like him," I suggest. "I doubt it's him."

She gives me a shrewd look. "I may be nearsighted, but I'm as sure that's your sculptor as I am that I'm not Aphrodite."

"What sculptor?" Nikomedes repeats, scowling slightly.

"It's not important," I insist.

"I thought you were such great friends," Zobia says. "Have you quarreled?"

"No, we haven't quarreled. I just don't think that's him."

"Would somebody please explain to me who the guy is?" Nikomedes asks.

I sigh. "Zobia thinks he looks like a sculptor we met at the temple of Athena Nike on the hill," I explain in a rush, hoping that will put an end to it.

"He looks like a slave," Nikomedes observes.

This annoys me. "Why do you say that?"

He shrugs. "Well, if he lives in the Ceramicus . . ."

"Maybe he was visiting a workshop."

I walk slower, hoping to increase the distance between Maron and us. He has long legs and should soon be safely out of range.

"So what did you quarrel about?" Zobia asks.

"I told you, we didn't quarrel!" I keep my voice low, not wanting Maron to hear us.

Then to my complete mortification, Nikomedes lets out an ear-splitting whistle that can be heard the length of the street. We all stop.

Of course Maron glances back to see what the commotion is. If I could duck behind a wall, I would, but he has seen us. He stops and waits for us to catch up. His face is impassive. He looks neither pleased nor displeased to see me. I think about how I will kill Nikomedes when we get home.

But for now I have no choice but to introduce him to Maron, although I would prefer not to. Nikomedes will ask too many questions, or he'll say something that will embarrass me. Maybe both. I can't believe this is happening.

"We're in a bit of a rush," I tell Maron.

He falls into step beside us, ignoring my hint. "I'm surprised to see you here. What brings you to the Ceramicus?"

"I had to see a friend." No need to give him details. It's not really any of his business.

"What about *you*?" Nikomedes demands. "What are you doing here?"

I can't believe how protective he sounds. I throw him a black look, but he doesn't notice.

"I live here," Maron says, not even glancing at him.

"Back there where we saw you coming out?"

I could kick him. I can't meet Maron's eyes, but I know he's looking at me. I hope he doesn't think I've been searching for him. This is just so awkward.

"So you have a friend who lives in the Ceramicus?" he asks me.

"Yes." I look straight ahead and try not to meet his eyes.

"And you were just making a social call, accompanied by your nurse and your cousin?"

"Yes." If I don't encourage him, perhaps he'll leave.

"I suppose you're very busy preparing for your wedding?"

Zobia stops abruptly in spite of our need for haste. This forces us all to stop.

"Young man, if you are in fact a friend of Rhea's, you know how little she's looking forward to this event. To suggest otherwise is just plain mean. Are you trying to be mean?"

I could hug her. All the world may be against me, but Zobia is on my side.

"No, I wasn't." Maron looks at me. "So why are you really here?"

I sigh. Why not just tell him? "If you must know, I was trying to find out where Euphrastus lives."

He raises an eyebrow. "And did you find out?"

"No."

"So now you're just giving up?"

"Uh, we really need to be getting back," Nikomedes interrupts. "There's no time for this."

"I didn't know who else to ask," I tell Maron.

"You could ask me."

We all stare at him in shocked silence. It didn't occur to me to ask Maron. I didn't think he even knew Euphrastus.

"You know where he lives?" I say when I find my voice.

His dark eyes bore into me. "I do, but first tell me why you want to know."

I swallow. "I want to persuade him to release me from the marriage arrangement."

"And what makes you think he will listen?"

"I don't know what else to do. I can't reason with my uncle. Maybe Euphrastus will take pity on me."

"Of course he will."

The sarcasm in his voice stops me cold. Am I the only one who thinks this might work? "So you won't tell me where he lives?"

"I'll tell you, but only on one condition."

"What's that?"

"You let me go with you."

I blink. I wasn't expecting that.

"I'm going with her," Nikomedes says.

"So am I," Zobia chimes in.

"My condition stands." He crosses his arms in front of his chest, his eyes never leaving mine.

So the only way I can find out where Euphrastus lives is if I agree to let Maron go there with me.

"Oh, very well," I say. "You can come too, but it has to be tonight. I'm running out of time. The wedding is only seven days away."

"All right," he says. "It's settled. I'll take you there. Where shall we meet—your house?"

I see the look of surprise on Nikomedes' face as he realizes Maron knows where I live. No doubt he's wondering just how well I know Maron.

"No," I say quickly. "By the statue of Hermes at the end of the street."

"At dusk?"

"No, after dark." I don't have the nerve to look at Nikomedes. Whatever he is thinking at least he keeps it to himself.

Having agreed upon this plan, we go our separate ways, Maron heading for the Acropolis, where his frieze waits, while we hurry toward the agora to purchase the figs we said we would buy.

When we arrive home, Kalchas is washing up in the courtyard. Nikomedes has not yet been missed, so he sneaks back into his room and climbs into bed without anyone realizing he has been gone. Kalchas didn't find his tablet at the school, but in the meantime it has mysteriously turned up near Nikomedes' schoolbag in the hall.

Our excursion has tired Zobia and so she trudges upstairs to take a nap. I'm nervous about my plan to confront Euphrastus and can't settle down to anything. In the loom room I keep getting my wool tangled as I try to spin it. At lunch I have no appetite. As the afternoon crawls by, I rehearse in my head what I'll say to Euphrastus. Supper comes and goes without Lycurgus making an appearance. No one comments on his absence. I wonder if he has gone back to the House of the Egyptian. Maybe the others are wondering the same.

As the household begins to retire, I decide it's time to wake Zobia. We should leave soon.

I shake her gently and she wakes. She seems confused.

"It's time to go," I whisper.

"Go?"

"To talk to Euphrastus."

"I'm so tired," she says. "I'm afraid you'll have to go without me."

I feel reluctant to leave her, but there is so little time left before the day that has been set for the wedding. I must talk to Euphrastus before it's too late.

With my mantle over my arm, I tiptoe downstairs as quietly as possible, hoping Kalchas will be sleeping so Nikomedes can make his escape. Nikomedes has made a remarkable recovery from his illness since our return earlier in the day, but Kalchas insists he rest and to be sure he does has stationed himself on a chair outside the room where Nikomedes lies. When he sees me, he scowls. My stomach drops.

"I just want to see how Nikomedes is doing," I say.

"The boy will live. He ate enough food tonight for several boys his size. I think he's well on the road to recovery. This was surely not the plague."

"May I see him?" I ask.

"No, he might still be sick enough to make you sick as well. You can see him tomorrow if he continues to improve. Now off with you."

I can't tell him that tomorrow will be too late. It has to be tonight. I wonder if Nikomedes is lying awake listening. Clearly he isn't going to give Kalchas the slip this time. As I retreat upstairs, I feel uneasy about my plan to visit Euphrastus. Circumstances are conspiring against me. I fear it's a sign that my efforts will come to nothing. Perhaps I should abandon my plan, but I told Maron I would meet him by the statue of Hermes at the end of the street. I have already disappointed him once, and I don't want to do it again. So I wait until I think Kalchas will be asleep, then with my sandals in hand steal downstairs to the door. I open it slowly, trying to make no noise, but just as I'm about to leave, I cast a glance toward Kalchas and see that he's watching me. I hold my breath, waiting for him to raise the alarm and get me in trouble. When he doesn't, I take a deep breath, step across the threshold, and close the door behind me. I have no idea why Kalchas didn't try to stop me, but there's no time to think about that now. Maron is waiting and I must hurry.

CHAPTER 25

I tell myself it's no different than the night I went to the amphitheater, but then why is my heart beating so wildly? I walk rapidly, worried that I'll be late. Soon I pass three men carrying torches and one calls after me, "What's the hurry, honey?" My heart is ready to burst by the time I reach the statue of Hermes, where Maron is waiting with a torch in his hand.

"You're alone?" he says, surprised, looking back up the dark street from where I've come.

"Zobia isn't feeling well," I explain breathlessly, "and Nikomedes couldn't get away."

He looks uncertain. "Are you sure you still want to do this?"

"Of course. Why do you even ask?"

He runs a hand through his hair. Surely he's not going to change his mind now. If he does, my plan will fall apart. If I show up at Euphrastus's house alone after dark, can I trust him to treat me civilly? Maron's eyes gleam in the moonlight as he considers. I hold my breath.

"All right then. Let's do this."

All my pent up tension ebbs away, replaced by relief.

The stars are coming out as we walk along the Street of Statues. Our torchlight catches the busts and effigies on their pedestals. Small groups of men pass us on their way home or to banquets, their torches growing brighter as they approach, then receding behind us. Some give us curious glances. I try to keep my face shadowed by my mantle.

"Who is your friend in the Ceramicus?" Maron asks as we walk. "The one you were visiting this morning."

"You mean Chloe? She's a flute girl who works for Aspasia, only now with Pericles ill she's staying with her music teacher."

"And how did you come to be friends with a flute girl?" he asks, a smile twitching at his lip.

"She was playing at one of my uncle's banquets and we got into a conversation when she wandered into the courtyard below my balcony."

"I don't suppose your uncle knows?"

"Of course not."

As our torch throws dancing shadows around us on the street, I remember how he kissed me after he walked me home from the amphitheater that night. Now seems like a good time to clear away any misunderstanding.

"About the other night—" I begin.

"Forget it. It was a foolish thing for me to do. I forgot myself."

"You know my uncle would never allow—"

"We both know what kind of man your uncle would choose for you."

Yes. Euphrastus. A man to whom he owes a gambling debt. A man who left his baby daughter to die on a mountainside. I clutch my mantle closer.

"What will you say to him when we get there?" Maron asks.

"I'll ask him to release me from the marriage arrangement."

"And if he refuses?"

"I'll plead with him. I'll get down on my knees if I have to."

"No, don't do that. You shouldn't have to beg."

"But I have to change his mind."

"If he's a decent man, he'll release you."

"If I thought he was a decent man, I wouldn't be so afraid of him."

Maron stops walking. "Maybe this is a bad idea."

But I can't turn back, not after coming this far. "Please," I say. "At least show me where he lives."

He looks sideways at me as we start walking again. "Where did you get such determination? You look like you were playing with dolls just yesterday."

"I suppose I was. But then the war came and this plague, and everything changed."

We pass by a statue with a broken arm. I look away, hoping it's not a bad omen.

"How do you know where he lives?" I ask, curious.

"I asked."

"Why would you do that?"

"Because I wanted to know."

He doesn't say it was because of me, but why else would he have done that? I'm about to ask him when he stops again. His torch throws our shadows on the wall beside us and I see a door. "This is it. Are you ready? Shall I knock?"

Suddenly I feel uncertain. Am I making a mistake? Even if I am, it's too late to worry about that now. I nod, not trusting myself to speak.

He lifts the knocker, then drops it. It bangs so loudly I think everyone in the street must have heard it. In the silence that follows it seems to echo.

Just as I begin to think no one will answer, the door opens and before us stands a sullen-looking woman with a bruise on her face. Her flat eyes slide over us distrustfully. "What do you want?"

I take a deep breath and step forward. "To speak with the master of the house."

"He doesn't like to be disturbed."

"It's important."

She looks from me to Maron. "What's it about? Do you owe him money?"

I stand straighter. "Please tell him Rhea, daughter of Theron, wishes to speak to him."

She looks Maron over again. "And who's he?"

"It would not have been proper or safe for me to come here alone at this hour," I explain.

She considers this, then grudgingly disappears within.

"Friendly," Maron mutters.

Soon she is back and this time she lets us in. We follow her into the house. It's bare and unwelcoming, with none of the homey touches of my uncle's house—no colorful wall hangings, no painted tiles on the floor, no decorative urns. She leaves us standing in the hall and we wait until Euphrastus comes. He's taller than I expected. The scar down his face is every bit as terrible as it looked that night in the moonlight when I watched him lumbering after Chloe in the courtyard below. He has a steep forehead, a bony lowering brow, bloodshot eyes, and a cruel mouth. He is bearded but not neatly like my uncle, and his hair is rumpled. Stinking of wine and sweat, he looks me over brazenly, as if I'm a slave girl he's considering buying.

"So you're my wife-to-be. You're scrawnier than I expected, but no matter. We'll fatten you up. Does your uncle know you're here?"

I lift my chin. "No. I came on my own."

"Did you now? Couldn't wait for the wedding?" He leers and takes a step closer.

Beside me Maron tenses. I know I should speak up before he says anything. He might make matters worse.

"I want you to release me from the marriage arrangement," I say and look Euphrastus straight in the eye, although I have to look up to do this since he towers over me. He is so close that I can smell his foul breath. He looks at me with contempt.

"And why would I do that?"

"Because I'd make you a terrible wife." I don't know where I find the courage to stand up to him. I just know I must not fail. Too much depends on this.

"Is that a fact?" He leers again.

Desperately I launch into the argument I have prepared

in my head. "I'm not skilled at the spindle or the loom. I have no idea how to manage servants. I can't cook."

He waves a hand dismissively. "You'll learn. And anyway my mother runs the household."

"Please," I say. "You can't possibly want me."

In a flash his face distorts with anger. He takes another step closer. I try not to cringe away. "You think this is about you? Well, this has nothing to do with you. It's between your uncle and me."

I stare at him. Nothing to do with me? What does he mean? My life is about to be ruined.

"This has everything to do with me," I say, trying to keep my voice steady. Anger gives me strength. "This is my future."

"Who cares about your future?" he sneers. "You'll learn soon enough to keep your mouth shut and do as you're told."

Desperate, I make one final attempt to reason with him. "Surely there are other women more suited to you."

"Your uncle owes me. Just ask him."

"I'll pay you," I tell him, hoping money might tempt him.

He grins and I notice he's missing a tooth. "How? When you're my wife, your money becomes my money. Would you bargain with money that will belong to me anyway?"

"You can have it. You're welcome to it. Just let me go."

"Why would I do that? Every man needs a woman to keep his bed warm and bear his children. Why not the niece of a councilman to bear my sons?"

"I'll die first."

"I doubt that. In fact, maybe you'll come to like it."

"Never."

He grins again and lays a hand on my arm. "We could find out right now."

Maron is between us in a flash with a knife pointed at Euphrastus's chin.

"What's this?" Euphrastus demands, frowning. "You dare to threaten me? In my own home?"

"You'll not lay a hand on her," Maron says.

"And who are you? One of Lycurgus's slaves? Did he send you to protect the merchandise?"

"Maybe."

"You understand this young wench will be my wife within a week? She'll be mine to do with as I please."

"That may be, but she's not your wife yet."

Euphrastus glares at him, but he doesn't back down. "Get out of here then, both of you. And you'd better watch your back, boy. A slave can get his throat cut on a dark night. You'd best remember that."

"So can an Athenian citizen," Maron replies evenly. "Now I think we're done here."

Without taking our eyes off Euphrastus, we retreat. The woman with the bruised face is lurking in the hall. I suspect she heard everything that was said. Her sullen eyes follow us as we leave, but she says nothing and makes no move to stop us.

When the door closes behind us, Maron bends down to tuck his knife into the sandal lacings that run up his leg, then picks up his torch.

"You can't marry that man."

"I know that."

Now that the ordeal is over, I feel shaken. Why did I think that talking to Euphrastus would do any good? It was a stupid idea.

"So what are you going to do?" Maron asks, glancing sideways at me as we head back to the Street of Statues.

"I don't know."

"Why would your uncle marry you to a man like that?" he asks in disgust.

"I told you. For a gambling debt."

"So you get punished for a lifetime just because he made a bad wager?"

"He probably thinks I'll adapt. Besides, I'm old enough to marry now. And with the war on and the plague . . . Well, he wants to be sure I'm taken care of. I don't think he realizes . . ." I stop. Why am I defending my uncle?

"You speak as if you're resigned to it. Are you?"

I shake my head. "Of course not."

"Then run away. Don't let your uncle do this to you."

"And where would I go? Who would take me in? As long as I'm in the city, he can find me, and then he'll force me to marry Euphrastus or sell me into slavery for disobeying him."

"Leave Athens," Maron says.

"How can I leave Athens? The Spartans have pulled back because of the plague, but they're still out there. What mercy can I expect from them?"

"Ships leave daily from Piraeus."

"I have no money for a passage."

"I could give you money."

I don't know what to say. I can't take money from Maron. Any money he has he has earned with the sweat of his brow and he is saving it to buy his freedom.

"Think about it," he says.

I nod, but I know I can't accept his offer. It isn't just the money. I'm not sure I could leave Athens, which is the only home I've ever known. All the world beyond its walls seems like a vast uncivilized wilderness. Is exile really the only way out of my dilemma?

As we pass the statue of Hermes on the corner of my uncle's street, I remember the kiss Maron gave me that night he walked me home from the amphitheater and wonder if he will kiss me again. I try to push the thought aside. Of course he won't. Not after the way I reacted the last time.

"Will you be all right?" he asks when the torchlight falls on my uncle's door. "You won't be punished for going out, will you?"

"No one knows I went out." Then I remember Kalchas sitting guard by Nikomedes' door.

"Not even that old nurse of yours? I'm surprised she let you out of her sight."

"She was tired."

He looks at me as if he wants to say more. Perhaps he's remembering that other night too.

"I suppose I should go in now," I say.

"I suppose so."

I wait to see if he will say anything else, but the silence draws itself out until I have no choice but to turn and go into the house.

Once inside, I see that Kalchas is still guarding

Nikomedes' room. He sits with his eyes closed and his head thrown back against the wall. I'll have to wait for tomorrow to speak to Nikomedes. I have my foot on the first step of the stairs when Kalchas says, "So you're back."

My heart sinks. "You won't tell, will you?" I ask in a low voice.

"If your uncle catches you, he'll beat you, you know." He too keeps his voice low.

"He won't find out unless you tell him."

"It's a dangerous game you're playing."

"It's not a game."

"I hope he's worth it. Now go on before your uncle comes home and finds you lurking about down here."

I realize he thinks I have been at a lovers' tryst. Maybe he pities me, knowing how soon I'll lose what little freedom I have. In any case I don't bother to deny it but hasten up the stairs. Once in my room, I fold my mantle and lay it in my chest. Then I cross the room to wake Zobia. I want to tell her all about my visit to Euphrastus with Maron. I want her to comfort me and tell me everything will be all right.

"Zobia," I whisper, kneeling by her bed.

Her only response is a sort of moan.

"What is it?" I ask, reaching for her hand.

I'm surprised at how warm it is. I touch her forehead. She's burning up with fever.

"Get Lede," she murmurs.

"No, I'll get Myrrine," I say, stumbling to my feet. I tell myself there's nothing to be alarmed about. It's only some passing illness. Nothing that a good rest won't cure. No reason to panic. It isn't the plague. There's no reason to fetch Lede.

"Get Lede," she repeats, her voice faint and raspy.

I hurry to the room where Lede and Myrrine sleep. They wake as I burst in.

"What is it?" asks Myrrine, sitting up. "What's wrong?"

"Zobia." It comes out almost a sob. "She's got a fever."

Myrrine swings her feet to the floor without a word.

"She said to get Lede." My voice quavers.

"It'll be all right," Myrrine says quietly as she pushes her long hair behind her shoulder. Lede rises without a word and reaches for her belt to cinch the waist of her tunic.

"You stay here," Myrrine tells me.

"No." I won't be shunted aside like a child. Zobia is a second mother to me. She's all I have left now.

"Then go fetch a cup of water," Myrrine says. "She'll be thirsty."

I fly down the stairs.

Kalchas' eyes snap open as I pass him. "What—?"

"Zobia's sick."

In the kitchen I dip a cup into the water pot. My hands are trembling. I pray silently to the gods. It can't be the plague. It just can't. Everybody else has been taken from me. I can't lose Zobia too.

When I return with the cup of water, Myrrine meets me at the door of my room and stops me from entering.

"I want to see her," I say, on the verge of tears. If only I had been home when she took ill. If only I had paid more attention to her. If only I had realized she was sick.

"You can't do anything for her." Myrrine gently takes the cup from my hands.

"If I were sick, she would take care of me."

"Yes, she would," Myrrine agrees. "But she would not want you to risk your life. Let Lede take care of her."

CHAPTER 26

My bed and chest have been moved to Myrrine's room. I prowl about restlessly, always ending up outside my old room, where Zobia lies ill. I blame myself for a hundred things. I should not have been so wrapped up in my problems that I did not notice she was ill. I should not have made her climb the Acropolis. I should have been kinder, gentler, more considerate. And now it's too late. I feel as if the gods are punishing me for my selfishness and pride. I alternate between praying to them and feeling angry at them. It's me who should have been punished, not her. She has never done anything wrong. She's as blameless as a child.

But the gods don't listen. Zobia dies two days later. On that same day Pericles dies and the whole city mourns. Women wail in the streets and pull their hair. Tradesmen close their shops. There are random acts of violence and rumors of unrest. The Assembly holds an emergency meeting at the Pnyx. No one knows what will happen next. Athens, the beating heart of the civilized world, suddenly seems on the brink of collapse.

Zobia's death leaves me numb. I have no interest in anything, not my scrolls or the fate of Athens. I'm useless in the loom room, where I just sit and cry. At times Myrrine loses patience with me, but mostly she takes it upon herself to see I eat something at meals and bathe and change my clothes.

Each day brings the day of my marriage closer, but I no longer care. It's on the second day after Zobia's burial when I hear raised voices as I pass my uncle's study on my way to fetch a cup of water for old Xantippe. I hear my name and stop to listen. Myrrine is arguing with my uncle about the marriage arrangement.

"Surely it could wait a little longer. She just lost Zobia. She's in no condition to celebrate a wedding."

But my uncle is as implacable as ever. "I've waited long enough. She's had plenty of time to prepare herself. Besides, this may be just what she needs. A change of scene. New responsibilities. A husband."

Myrrine tries again. "What would it hurt to wait a week or two, or even a month? Give her time to mourn."

"She'll marry when I decide," my uncle declares. "There's been enough waiting."

"You may push her to do something desperate," Myrrine warns.

"Enough. Get back to work. I don't want to hear any more of this."

Myrrine is frowning as she emerges from his study.

When she sees me standing there holding Xantippe's cup, she hesitates.

I don't want her to feel bad. "It's all right," I tell her. "It doesn't matter. Nothing matters now."

"That's not true." She comes closer and touches my arm. "This isn't you speaking, Rhea. It's your grief."

Maybe. But how can I separate myself from my grief? I have lost Zobia and nothing will ever be the same. "You told me I should just accept. Remember? It's what the gods have decreed."

"I don't believe that anymore. I've changed my mind. You deserve more than this."

"I have no choice. You heard my uncle."

"You *do* have a choice," she says fiercely, her hand gripping my arm as if she will force me to feel. "Don't you ever forget that."

I wait until she lets go, then continue on my way to the kitchen and dip the cup into the water pot. I feel only numbness about the approaching marriage. What difference does it make if I live in my uncle's house or that of Euphrastus? When I'm gone, someone else will take old Xantippe her cup of water. She probably won't even notice I'm gone. She'll just start calling someone else Nysa.

Since Zobia's death, I like to sit in old Xantippe's room and listen to her talk. She expects nothing of me except to fetch her water. And after she falls asleep I often sit with her in the dark listening to her snore. That's where I am when Myrrine comes in later.

"Here you are," she says. "Why are you sitting in the dark? Never mind. Go get your mantle. We're going out."

"At night? Why?"

"Someone wants to talk to you."

"Who?" I don't really feel like going out. It seems like too much trouble. I'm reluctant to leave the comfort of Xantippe's dark room, like a small furry animal curled up in its hole.

"Come and you'll find out," Myrrine says.

"A man or a woman?" I only ask because it delays the moment of rising. I suspect she has fabricated the story of a visitor just to get me out of the house. It's ironic. Before, everyone wanted me to stay inside, and now Myrrine has taken to thinking of reasons why I should go out.

"Would you keep your visitor waiting?" she asks.

If I really do have a visitor, who could it be? Chloe? Would she have risked the dangers of the streets to come to my uncle's house at night? Or could it be a message from Aspasia? Maybe she has sent word that she has found a way to stop my marriage now that it no longer matters.

"Why didn't you invite this visitor in?" I ask.

"Perhaps the message is private," Myrrine says. "Now are you going to sit here in the dark or are you going to get your mantle?"

If it's a slave with a message from Aspasia, it wouldn't be polite to keep him waiting. Maybe it's old Nestor. In that case I will have to tell him I'm grateful to Aspasia but it's too late. It doesn't matter now. Sighing, I get up. Old Xantippe goes on snoring, oblivious of us. I envy her ability to lose herself in sleep.

With Myrrine hovering over me, I fetch my mantle from the room we share. She drapes hers over her head at the same time.

"You're coming too?" I ask, surprised.

"Of course, silly goose. You didn't think I'd let you go out alone after dark, did you?"

"I'm sure I'd be safe. It's just outside the door, right?"

"You are not going out alone," she says firmly.

It doesn't seem worth arguing about so I let the matter drop.

When we get downstairs, there is no sign of my uncle so I assume he has gone out. Perhaps he is at the House of the Egyptian or perhaps he is at a banquet. Kalchas emerges from his room as we head for the door. I expect him to demand to know where we are going, but he just nods to Myrrine without a word. Now that's strange. Does he know what this is about? Myrrine gives me no time to ask more questions, just hustles me out the door.

Once outside, I look about but the dark street is deserted. "Where is this mysterious visitor?" I ask, puzzled.

"Waiting for us at the temple of Apollo."

This too seems strange. Could Aspasia herself have come to see me? If she did, she might want to avoid my uncle and the little temple is near—not more than a short walk away. But Myrrine still refuses to explain.

So we set off in the direction of the temple, walking briskly. We pass a noisy group of men on their way home from a banquet and several solitary walkers. Overhead clouds scud across the pale moon.

As we near the small temple of Apollo, I see a man with a torch sitting on the steps but no sign of Aspasia. He might be her servant, but when we draw closer, he stands and I see that it's Maron.

"Go on," Myrrine says, giving me a gentle push.

"I don't understand."

"Just listen to what he has to say."

I'm surprised Myrrine has tricked me into meeting Maron. If my uncle finds out, we'll both be in trouble. I'm practically a married woman and I should not be sneaking out to meet another man under cover of dark.

"You came," Maron says when I reach him. He sounds as if he doubted that I would.

"Why are you here?" I ask.

It seems like ages since we last spoke, but it's been just five days since we went to confront Euphrastus. In that time Zobia has died and my life has changed completely. He's a part of my past now, not of my bleak present or my even bleaker future.

"I heard about what happened to Zobia," he says. "I'm sorry."

I nod, not trusting myself to speak.

"And your marriage?"

"Two days away."

He reaches for my hand. I wasn't expecting that. It sends a shiver through me, but I let him hold it. His hand feels large and reassuring. But no one can stop the inevitable.

"Don't do this. Please, Rhea." His eyes are pleading.

I glance over my shoulder. Myrrine has stationed herself discretely out of earshot. She is standing guard on the path that leads to the temple. There is no one else around. In the distance I hear a dog barking.

"I have to," I tell him. "It's too late now."

"It's not too late."

"Everything's been arranged."

"Why are you doing this?" he demands. "Is it because of Zobia?"

"It has nothing to do with Zobia," I say calmly. "My uncle is my guardian. I have to do what he says."

"You know that isn't true." His eyes gleam and his face looks different in the flickering light of the torch, leaner, bolder. "You're just doing this because you blame yourself for Zobia's death. You're punishing yourself."

This seems unfair. Why doesn't everybody stop trying to interfere? I feel exhausted. I just want to curl up in a ball and sleep for a very long time.

"Don't you see I have to marry him? I have no choice."

"No, I don't see," he says angrily. "You do have a choice. You could run away."

But I can't. I have no place to go. Or is he suggesting I go with him?

"With you?"

"Yes, with me. Or alone. Just so long as you don't marry Euphrastus."

I want to comfort him, but I don't know how. I feel so tired.

"They would catch us," I say patiently, as if explaining to a child. "They would bring us back. I would have to marry Euphrastus anyway. They would beat you or worse. Don't you see it wouldn't work?"

Maron touches my cheek. "How long do you think you'll survive married to a man like that? He'll beat you — you know he will. He'll crush your spirit and he'll break your body. And when he's done, you'll be dead, or at least some part of you will be."

"What does it matter? We're all going to die."

"We could leave here."

I shake my head. "This is my home. This is where I belong. This is all I've ever known."

"It will never be the same again. Athens will lose this war. Even if it goes on for years, and it may, in the end Athens will lose. It was a mistake to ever start fighting Sparta, one that will cost this city dearly."

"You can't know that." I pull my hand away and take a step back. I don't want to hear him say these things. I don't want to believe Athens can be defeated. Surely the gods will not let this happen. Surely Athena will protect us.

"Open your eyes. Just look around you. The truth of what I say is all around you."

"No, it can't be the end. Athens will go on."

"It'll go on, but it will never again be as great as it was before. The glory that was Athens will be gone. Reality will be something else entirely. The Athenians will be a conquered people."

I shake my head, refusing to believe it. "I have to go now."

"So this is good-bye?"

"I guess so."

He nods. "All right then. If you're sure I can't change your mind . . . But if you ever need help, I will try to help you. You'll remember that, won't you?"

I blink back my tears. I hope I will see him again, but I know I might not. I might spend the rest of my days a prisoner in my husband's house. Some women live like that. I try to memorize Maron's face so I will never forget it—

those dark intelligent eyes, the chiseled lines of his cheekbones, his strong jaw. Then I walk away without looking back. I know he's watching me, and I'm afraid my resolution may crumble if I look back. I can't run away with Maron. If I did, we would both be fugitives, but the penalty for being caught would be far worse for him than for me. He might have to pay with his life, and I'm not going to let him do that.

Myrrine's hopeful expression fades as I approach.

"What did he say?" she asks as we start down the dark street, her arm linked in mine.

"He asked me to run away with him."

"And you turned him down?"

"Yes."

"He loves you, you know."

I don't say anything. Surely she sees I can't run away with him. He's a slave. We would have no place to go. The Scythian guard would hunt us down.

She sighs heavily.

"How did you know about Maron?" I ask.

"Zobia told me."

I'm surprised. I always thought Zobia kept my secrets. But now that I think about it, of course she would have talked about me to Myrrine.

"What did she tell you about him?" I ask, curious.

"She said he was a nice enough young man, but a slave, which made him totally unsuitable, and so of course you promptly imagined you were in love with him."

"It wasn't like that," I protest. "We're just friends."

Myrrine shrugs. "When he showed up tonight and

wanted to speak to you, I thought maybe he could talk some sense into you, but I guess I was wrong."

If she had told me it was Maron who wanted to see me instead of spiriting me through the streets with so much secrecy, I could have told her it would do no good. It would change nothing. Nobody can save me now. My future is plotted out. I will be Euphrastus's wife and bear his children. Unless of course I die of the plague or Athens loses its war with Sparta.

"Do you think the Spartans will win this war?" I ask her.

"I don't know. If you had asked me before, I would have said no, but now that Pericles is dead . . ." She shakes her head.

Somewhere a dog barks. A cloud passes in front of the moon.

"Do you think the gods are punishing us?"

"For what?"

"For starting this war."

"I don't worry about such things. I just try to stay out of trouble and get my work done."

"But you believe in the gods, don't you?"

"Of course, I do. What a question."

"Are you angry at them for making you a slave?"

"No, that was just bad luck. My island was captured by the Athenians. My people were enslaved."

"But your people lost because the gods favored the Athenians," I point out.

"No, the Athenians had better trained soldiers and bigger ships. That's why we lost." She says it matter-of-factly. Could she be right that the gods had nothing to do with it? And if it was true for her island, could it also be true for Athens? Might Sparta win because it has better trained soldiers? And if it does, what will become of the people of Athens?

"Aren't you worried about what will happen to us if the Spartans win this war?" I ask.

"I don't suppose it will be a lot different for me. A master is a master."

It might not make a difference for her, but for me it could make a world of difference. For a moment I wonder if I've made a mistake turning down Maron's offer to run away with him, but the forces opposed against us are so formidable that escape seems impossible. Isn't it better to resign myself to what the gods have decreed?

Later, stretched out on my narrow bed, I find it hard to fall asleep. Perhaps seeing Maron has disturbed me more than I realize. I toss and turn and argue with him in my head. When this has been going on for a while, I glance over at Myrrine's bed and notice it's empty. Maybe she has gone to check on old Xantippe. I get up and walk out on the balcony. The moon is shining down into the courtyard, making it an enchanted place of light and shadow. I remember the night of my uncle's last banquet when I looked down on Chloe and Euphrastus in the moonlit courtyard, a nymph and a bear. How long ago it seems now! How much older I feel. I was so determined to avoid my fate and now I accept it. I was a child then, and now I'm a woman. Dear old Zobia was alive then and now she is gone forever, a shade in the underworld with the other shades of those I loved.

I'm immersed in these gloomy thoughts when a movement in the shadows below catches my eye and I snap to attention. Is it a trick of the moonlight? Isn't everyone sleeping? Then I see it again. A large shadow near one of the columns moves slightly. I look harder. Could an animal have gotten into the courtyard? Again it moves. What is it? Not an animal. A person. No, two people locked in an embrace. They make no sound. I draw back so they won't see me. Who are they? If only they would step into the moonlight so I could see them better! I remember Myrrine's empty bed. Has she slipped out to meet a lover? Surely she wouldn't take such a risk. If caught, she could be beaten, perhaps sold. I can't imagine Myrrine with a lover, and yet that must be her. Then like a thunderbolt it hits me that the man with her is Kalchas. All the pieces fall into place—glances exchanged, whispered words, Myrrine urging me not to get Kalchas into trouble. Why didn't I see it before? How blind I have been!

I slip back into the room and climb back into bed. I won't give her away. Now I understand why she changed her mind about my marriage to Euphrastus. Her feelings for Kalchas have made her think differently. I have no idea what future she imagines they could have. She knows how the odds are stacked against them, yet she chooses to risk everything. She's so much braver than I am. I envy her, for although a slave, she has found love, and that is something I will never know.

CHAPTER 27

Even prisoners condemned to die get a last request before drinking the hemlock. So should I. With this in mind I seek out Nikomedes in the dining room when I go down for breakfast. He's reclining on a couch biting into a chunk of bread spread with honey when I walk up to him.

"Suppose a girl likes a boy . . . ," I begin.

"What?" He almost chokes and his eyes fly about the room in alarm. Kalchas has not yet come in. Myrrine and Lede are setting out figs for Lycurgus on a platter beside his couch and are paying no attention to us. I know I shouldn't be here. I should be in the courtyard, where the women take breakfast. Lycurgus will be upset if he walks in and sees me here. But if that happens, I will say I'm helping Myrrine and Lede set out the food.

"Suppose a girl likes a boy," I repeat, "but he doesn't know she likes him, and she wants to let him know. And time is running out."

"Why is time running out?" Nikomedes asks with a scowl.

"It just is," I say, dismissing his interruption with a wave of my hand. "So what should she do?"

"Tell him," he mumbles.

"But she never has an opportunity to talk to him."

"She could send him a message." His eyes flick furtively around the room again.

"But she wants to tell him in person. Before it's too late."

He nods. "She could send a message saying she would like to meet him. She could tell him where to meet her."

I think about this. Would it work? Would Doros come if I sent him a message asking him to meet me?

"If I give you a message, would you give it to him?" I ask in a whisper.

"Give it to who?" He knits his brow in puzzlement.

"To Doros," I say impatiently. Who did he think I meant?

"You were talking about yourself?" He looks disappointed.

"Of course. Who else would I be talking about?"

"But you're going to be married tomorrow," he objects.

"So? I'm not married yet."

"What if someone finds out?"

I look at him. What do I care if someone finds out? What could anyone do to me aside from beating me or forcing me to marry Euphrastus? What's the worst that can happen? "Will you do it or not?"

He hesitates, watching Myrrine and Lede. "I will if you do something for me."

"What?"

"Deliver a message for me."

It's my turn to be mystified. "To who?"

He reddens and glances about. "Chloe, of course."

I don't know what I was expecting him to say but not that. Even if I agree to deliver a message for him, how can I go out now that I no longer have Zobia to chaperone me? If I go, I will have to go alone. And even if I can deliver it, is that a good idea? His father would not be happy if he found out. He and Chloe are from different worlds. And would she even agree? She might simply laugh at him for his infatuation. Or suppose she didn't laugh. Suppose she fell in love and he broke her heart. Or she broke his. Either way it would be my fault. I know I should refuse.

"Deal?" Nikomedes asks nervously.

I hesitate a moment longer. I can't very well turn him down if I expect him to deliver my message to Doros. Fair is fair. I have to agree to his terms and just hope neither Chloe nor Nikomedes gets hurt.

"Deal," I agree.

I wait until Lycurgus leaves for the agora before I sneak out of the house. With luck Myrrine may not even notice I'm gone. She and Lede are so tired of seeing me weeping and looking miserable that they are probably relieved when I choose not to join them in the loom room. And Myrrine feels so badly about the upcoming marriage that she's willing to turn a blind eye to almost anything I do, as long as Lycurgus doesn't find out. I still have to be careful of ruffians who might harass a young woman walking the streets alone, but it's becoming more common to see women in the streets since a number of men have died of the plague or fallen in skirmishes with the Spartans.

I make my way through the narrow winding streets, now familiar with the route that will take me to the house of Chloe's music teacher in the Ceramicus. When I rap on the door of the modest mud-brick house, it's answered by a female slave. I ask for Chloe, but instead I get her music teacher, a scowling dark-browed woman.

"What do you want, girl?" she asks sharply. "What business do you have with my pupil?"

"I have a message for her."

"What message?"

"I'm to give it to no one but her."

"That's ridiculous." She frowns and stares at me. "Is it from Aspasia?"

I don't answer. I'm not about to give Nikomedes' message to this harpy. Chloe may never get it. Let the woman think it's from Aspasia.

"Oh, very well, I'll get the girl," she snaps and abruptly leaves me standing there.

Moments later Chloe appears, delighted to see me. Her smile makes up for the chilly reception I received from her music teacher.

"You came alone?" She glances past me at the street, as if expecting to see someone standing there.

"Zobia's gone. She died three days ago of the plague." It's still hard to say it and tears spring to my eyes.

"I know." She hugs me. "Aspasia sent word."

I'm surprised Aspasia knows of my loss, especially when she has just suffered such a terrible loss of her own.

"Is she all right?" I ask.

"She hasn't caught the plague yet," Chloe says. "She's in mourning of course. Pericles was the love of her life."

"What will happen to her now?"

"I don't know, but hopefully her wealth and her friends will protect her from his enemies. What about you? What's to become of you?"

"I'm to be married tomorrow."

A look of dismay crosses her face. "You couldn't get out of it?"

I shake my head. "No." I don't really want to talk about it so I rush on to the purpose of my visit.

"I have a message for you."

"For me? What is it?"

"It's from Nikomedes, my cousin."

Her eyes grow wider. "Really?"

"He wants to know if you can meet him this afternoon in the agora." I say it in a rush of words and avoid her eyes. "You don't have to," I add quickly, not wanting her to feel obligated because he's my cousin.

"Oh, but I want to. Tell him yes. I'll be there."

"What about your music teacher?"

She wrinkles her nose. "I'll think of something. I'm very good at giving her the slip."

"You know you can't marry him," I warn her. "His father would never permit it."

"I don't expect to marry him. Boys like him don't marry flute girls. I know that. But he's ever so nice. He's sweet, you

215

know. All I ever meet are old men who want to paw me."
She shudders.

"He's very shy."

"So am I." She lifts her chin as if she thinks I might
disagree.

"What about that boy you said you were in love with?" I
ask her. "The most handsome in all of Athens."

She sighs. "He doesn't know I exist. Anyway he was just
a fantasy of mine—your cousin is real."

I bite my lip, debating whether to ask. "Was it Doros?"

She gives me a dimpled smile. "I thought you fancied
him too. Well, some other lucky girl will get him now."

"Yes."

I don't tell her I may be meeting him this very evening if
Nikomedes has delivered my message.

CHAPTER 28

From my perch on my balcony I wait for the sun to sink lower in the sky. If all goes according to plan, I will meet Doros at the Temple of Hephaestus at sunset. Nikomedes has delivered my message. I have prayed to Aphrodite that Doros will come. This is my last chance to speak to him before I am Euphrastus's wife.

When it's time, I steal down the stairs. The hall is empty and I slip out the door unnoticed. With my mantle draped over my head, I hurry through the streets, almost running. There are other people out returning from work or from the agora. Some glance at me curiously. I keep my head down and don't make eye contact. I don't want to arrive too late, nor do I want to arrive too early. I chose the Temple of Hephaestus because it's the perfect place from which to watch the sunset. It stands on a hill overlooking the agora, surrounded by pleasant gardens with date trees and songbirds. To my relief the sun is just setting when I climb the hill and enter the gardens, and the sky burns red through the stately temple columns. As I draw near, I see Doros sitting casually on the steps, one knee raised, gazing at the setting sun.

He looks so handsome that it takes my breath away. I glance about to see if his pedagogue is nearby, but we are alone, which is just as well since I doubt I'd have the nerve to approach him otherwise. Seeing him silhouetted against the red sky, an athletic young man in an attitude of repose, I could swear Apollo has appeared before me. A line from Sappho springs to mind: *Like to the gods he seems to me . . .*

At the sound of my footsteps he turns. Blue eyes meet mine. The sun's last rays set fire to his blonde curls. He smiles. "Hullo there."

I let my mantle fall back. Now that we're face-to-face, I feel suddenly shy. What do I say to him? *Aphrodite, give me words!*

"Are you alone?" he asks, looking beyond me at the gardens.

Did he expect me to bring a chaperone? Will he think I'm too bold because I've come alone?

"You aren't afraid of ruffians?"

I shake my head. I could tell him I would brave a dozen ruffians for the chance to be here with him. I have waited so long for this moment and can hardly believe it's finally here. I sit down on the nearest step but not too close. I don't want him to think I'm brazen. I used up all my courage when I sent Nikomedes with my message for him to meet me here.

"Have I seen you somewhere before?" he asks. "You look familiar."

"I saw you on the Acropolis," I say, finding my voice. "You were there to make offerings to the gods."

"Oh, the day before the races. Did you see them?"

"No."

"I won."

"Yes, I know."

"It was a good race. A shame you missed it."

"I wanted to see it, but my aunt and uncle wouldn't permit me."

"Oh, right." He seems to remember that young unmarried women are not supposed to watch young men compete nude.

"My brother liked to race."

"Did he? Who's your brother? Maybe I know him."

"He died of the plague three months ago."

"Sorry. Bad luck that."

"My father and mother died too." I don't know why I'm telling him this. It wasn't what I meant to say. I should not have mentioned the plague. What was I thinking? We have so little time. I must not waste a single moment of it. There is so much I want to tell him. But where do I start?

I take a deep breath. "I just wanted . . ." The words trail away. I don't want to tell him about Euphrastus or that I will marry tomorrow. How do I explain why I wanted him to meet me here?

He looks at me as if he's waiting for me to continue. Then he glances behind me. I turn to see if someone is standing there, but we are alone.

"I'm waiting for someone," he explains.

This confuses me. Doesn't he realize I sent the message

that brought him here? I told Nikomedes not to mention my name. It had seemed more romantic and mysterious just to say 'someone will be waiting for you at the Temple of Hephaestus at sunset.' I thought he would know I was the one who sent the message.

"I'm the one you're waiting for," I tell him.

"You must have me mixed up with someone else."

I don't know what to say. Of course I don't have him mixed up with someone else. How could I possibly mix him up with someone else?

Again he glances behind me. This time his face lights with a smile. I whirl about to see who is there. A man with hair beginning to grey lopes up the steps grinning and out of breath.

"Polybius!"

"Doros." The older man lays a hand on his shoulder. "I'm glad you could come." He looks at me. "And who might this be?"

"I didn't catch your name," Doros says.

They both look at me. I feel acutely the awkwardness of the situation. I have made a terrible mistake. In all my dreaming about this moment it never occurred to me that Doros wouldn't know me, but that's exactly what has happened. He has no idea who I am. I'm just a girl he met at the Temple of Hephaestus as the sun is setting. He probably doesn't remember seeing me that day at the Acropolis either. I'm nothing to him. Polybius is who he was waiting for and the reason he has ditched his pedagogue. And what of my message? Did he assume it was from his admirer, or did they arrange the meeting some other way? It doesn't really matter. The point is he's here to meet Polybius, not me. I'm disappointed and embarrassed. I wish the earth would open and swallow me. How could I have been so wrong?

I feel like a fool. Yes, he's as gorgeous as a god, but he has eyes only for Polybius. I might as well be one of the stone nymphs in the garden with finches perching on my outstretched hand. Blinded by tears, I turn and run out of the gardens and down the hill, and I don't stop until I'm back to my uncle's house.

Nikomedes must have been listening for me to come in because he bounds out of his room and stops me before I reach the stairs. He's leaning on a crutch.

"What happened to you?" I ask.

He grins. "Kalchas thinks I sprained my ankle."

"Did you?"

"No, but I had to have an excuse to get rid of him so I could meet Chloe in the agora."

"How did that get rid of him?"

"Simple. He had to go find a crutch. He couldn't very well carry me all the way home, could he?"

I roll my eyes. "So how did it go?"

"Great. Next time we're going to meet at the Monument to the Heroes. How about you? How did it go with Doros?"

"I shouldn't have gone. It was a mistake."

"Why? Was he rude?"

"No. Nothing like that. There was a man there."

"Polybius?"

I stare at him. "You knew about him?"

"I've seen them. Polybius is always hanging about."

"Why didn't you tell me?"

He shrugs. "I thought you knew."

"Nikomedes!" Kalchas' voice booms from the dining room.

"I have to go," Nikomedes says. "I'm supposed to be studying." He careens away on his crutch.

When I get upstairs, I sit down on my bed and hug myself. I feel as if my life is over. There's nothing more to look forward to. All my dreams about Doros are dashed. As Chloe said, he was a fantasy. And now that the fantasy is gone, I feel empty.

I'm still sitting on my bed, feeling defeated, when Myrrine breezes in.

"Where have you been?" she asks. "Did you go out?"

One look at my face and she sits down beside me on the bed and takes my hand. "What's wrong?"

Throwing my arms around her neck, I burst into tears and tell her everything.

At supper every bite I put in my mouth is hard to swallow. The voices of Myrrine and Lede seem too loud and too cheerful. They are doing their best to make me feel better, but all I can think about — besides the fiasco of my meeting with Doros — is that tomorrow I must marry Euphrastus.

After supper they carry water upstairs for my bridal bath. I submit because there no longer seems to be any point in fighting my fate. As a symbol that I'm leaving childhood behind, I hand Myrrine an old doll I brought from home and a tunic I have outgrown, offerings for Artemis, the virgin goddess. Myrrine snips a lock of my hair for Athena. Another pointless ritual.

Who would have thought the night before marriage could be so joyless? I just want to cry. If only Zobia and my mother were here to tell me everything will be all right. I think I would hold them and never let them go. This must be how Persephone felt, wrenched from her mother and forced into marriage with the dark Lord of the Underworld.

When everyone else has gone to bed, I lie awake, unable to sleep. The light of the full moon steals in from my balcony, making my room brighter than usual. It's the last night I will sleep under my uncle's roof. At this time tomorrow I'll be a married woman in my husband's house. My new life as the wife of Euphrastus will begin. I can't imagine how I'll endure it.

CHAPTER 29

When morning comes I want to stay in bed, but Myrrine won't allow it.

"Up, up, up," she says when it's barely dawn.

I groan and curl myself into a ball.

"Time to get up," she insists. "There's a lot to do. You can lie abed after you're a married woman. That is, if your husband will let you."

I can't imagine lying abed in that house with the bleak walls and sparse furnishings. Just the thought of it makes me want to burrow back under my blanket.

But I know Myrrine will torment me until I am up, so reluctantly I rise, splash myself with water from the basin, and head downstairs, where I listlessly eat a fig.

Instead of retiring to the loom room after breakfast, Myrrine and Lede rush about decorating the house with garlands of olive and laurel leaves in preparation for the wedding feast. It will be a small affair, not like the large feasts of former times, but the smell of baking sesame cakes wafts from the kitchen. Any other day I would love that smell but not today when it only serves to remind me that the long dreaded day of my wedding has arrived.

By mid-morning I'm dressed in a long purple tunic and Myrrine has braided a gold ribbon in my hair. I'm wearing silver earrings, a silver brooch on my shoulder, and a gold band on my arm. By midday the guests begin to arrive. From my balcony I can hear them talking and laughing. They are friends of my uncle's and relatives of my aunt's. Isn't it funny how you can be surrounded by people and still feel utterly alone? I'm supposed to stay in my room until Euphrastus arrives, but when he fails to appear by midafternoon, Myrrine comes to fetch me. Euphrastus is late, but my uncle wants me at the feast. He has paid for the food and he doesn't want Euphrastus to detract from his reputation as a host by showing up at the last minute to spirit me away. Myrrine explains this as she drapes the bridal veil over my face and lays a garland of violets on my head to hold it in place. When she finishes, she steps back to admire her handiwork.

"It's a shame your mother couldn't be here to see you."

At mention of my mother my tears begin to flow. It's as if they have been waiting just behind my eyes and this is their cue.

"Oh, please don't cry," Myrrine says, wringing her hands. "Your wedding feast is supposed to be a happy occasion."

I wipe my tears away with my fingers and get myself under control again.

She studies me anxiously. "Now are you ready to go down?"

I will never be ready, but sooner or later I have to face the wedding guests, so I nod. I concentrate on not tripping as we descend the stairs. Between the veil and my tears, everything is blurred. When I enter the banquet room, the guests fall silent for a few seconds, then burst into noisy chatter again. Myrrine leads me to the women's side of the room and seats me on a chair by a small table.

The guests have already started eating and now I'm expected to eat too. I try half-heartedly to nibble at some dates and nuts. I'm grateful for the veil. It hides the tears in my eyes and saves me from having to answer awkward questions.

"What's keeping the groom?" asks a man on the other side of the room. "He's missing his own wedding feast. Did he forget what day it is?" Some of the other men laugh.

It would be fine with me if he never shows up. I'm not looking forward to the torchlight procession to his house nor to what will take place afterward.

I look at the women around me. While they clucked over me when I first sat down, they have quickly forgotten about me. But I don't mind since that means I don't have to make small talk. I can just sit quietly with my own thoughts as the conversations swirl about me.

My uncle seems to have already imbibed a large quantity of wine. His voice is loud as he tells a bald man what will happen now that Pericles is gone.

"Of course the war will go on," my uncle declares. "Sparta will not make peace without a full-scale surrender, and the citizens of Athens will never agree to that."

"It's a shame he got us into this war," the bald man says. "If he had just been willing to compromise a little, we might not be in this mess."

Myrrine is refilling wine cups. She gives me an encouraging smile and a pat on the shoulder as she passes. In a corner of the room Nikomedes is fielding questions from two men standing on either side of him. One asks about his prowess with the discus and the other what he knows of the new philosophies being espoused at the gymnasiums these days. He says the discus is not really his strong point and the philosophies only make sense until the next philosopher demolishes them. The first answer doesn't surprise me, but the second does. I had no idea Nikomedes knew anything about philosophy.

Myrrine is coming by again when Kalchas appears in the doorway. He goes straight to Lycurgus and whispers in his ear.

"I must excuse myself for a few minutes," Lycurgus announces to the room at large. "A small matter has come up which requires my attention. Please continue without me. I shall return shortly." Then he leaves, followed by Kalchas. The guests resume eating and talking.

I wonder what has called my uncle away. As the minutes slip by and he doesn't return, I keep glancing at the door. I have a feeling something is wrong. If I were not wearing a purple tunic and a veil, I would jump up and go find out what's happening, but dressed as I am, I would attract too much attention. So I just sit here like an ornamental statue and wait while the noise of a dozen conversations surrounds me like the senseless buzzing of bees.

It seems ages before Lycurgus returns. When he does, he holds up his hands to silence the room. Everyone looks at him and conversation dies away. Myrrine pauses with the wine krater in her hands.

"I regret to say there will be no wedding today," my uncle announces, then pauses dramatically. "It seems the groom has been murdered."

If he intended to shock his guests, he has succeeded. There is a universal gasp, and then everyone begins to talk at once. I am surrounded by pandemonium. Euphrastus murdered? Is it possible?

"You might as well enjoy the food," my uncle says, raising his voice above the din. "It's a shame for all this to go to waste."

"Murdered?" people say. "How was he murdered?"

"Stabbed, I believe the messenger said." My uncle seems a bit distracted but not exactly distraught. "And on his wedding day!" He shakes his head in disbelief. Maybe it occurs to him that he is not showing sufficient sympathy, given the situation. "Awful thing," he mutters. "Shocking. We're none of us safe in our homes anymore."

"Was he murdered at home?" someone calls across the room, one of the men who was interrogating Nikomedes, I think.

"Yes, I believe so. They said his servants found him. He'd been stabbed a number of times. Repeatedly." My uncle drinks from his wine cup, as if to steady himself. He almost looks as if he's struggling not to laugh.

Meanwhile, I sit here amid the uproar trying to comprehend what has happened. One thing seems clear. I won't have to marry Euphrastus. Not today or any day. I've been saved by some weird twist of fate. The gods have taken pity on me.

Around me women chatter excitedly, and no one pays any attention to me. They are too busy talking to each other.

"Who murdered him?" someone asks my uncle.

"I have no idea," my uncle says. "Maybe it was a thief. Yes, I expect it was a thief. There's been a lot of that going on lately."

"One of these refugees," suggests another man. Other voices chime in, agreeing.

"Athens has more criminals and lowlifes than you can shake a stick at," says another. "It's a disgrace. Since this plague started, things have only gotten worse. People have no respect for the law anymore."

Myrrine bends down and whispers in my ear, "Are you all right?"

I nod. She sets a piece of sesame cake in front of me. My mother used to bake them as a special treat. I know it's wrong of me to feel glad about the death of Euphrastus, but it's as if an enormous weight has been lifted. Suddenly I have my life back.

Gradually the women remember I'm sitting here and take turns offering their condolences. I'm glad then for the veil because under it I can't stop smiling.

"Never mind, dear," says the lady beside me, patting my hand. "Your uncle will find a new husband for you in no time."

I could tell her I'm in no hurry, but I refrain. All that matters right now is that I have just been saved from a marriage to a man I loathed.

"Perhaps he'll marry the girl himself now that he's a widower," says another woman. "It would keep her father's property in the family."

I glance across the room at Lycurgus in alarm. Marry my uncle? That would be almost as bad as marrying Euphrastus. True, my uncle isn't a monster like Euphrastus, and he made my aunt happy enough, but I'm not my aunt. Surely he would want a woman who is good at managing the household, not an inexperienced girl of fifteen who prefers to curl up with a scroll of poetry. But such marriages among relatives to hold on to property are not uncommon. And my uncle is no longer a married man. There is nothing to stop him from doing this. In fact, the more I think about it, the more likely it seems. Suddenly I feel as if the room is closing in on me. The walls seem to tilt alarmingly. As if sensing my distress, Myrrine is at my side in a flash.

"Poor thing," she says to the women as she helps me stand. "It's an awful shock."

The women cluck sympathetically. Myrrine guides me out of the crowded room as if I'm a blind woman, which in a way I am since I can see only dimly through the veil. Even on the stairs, she steadies me with an arm around my waist. Not until I'm safely back in my room does she release me.

"Well, it seems you're not to be a bride today after all," she says.

I pull off the veil and my garland of violets falls to the floor. She reaches down to pick it up.

"You don't think my uncle will want to marry me, do you?" I ask nervously.

"I'm sure I have no idea. I just wish he wouldn't appear quite so pleased that Euphrastus is dead."

"Well, I'm pleased too," I tell her. "He was a terrible man and I'm glad I don't have to marry him."

"That may be, but it's a wicked thing to take delight in the death of another. The poor man was murdered. I doubt he deserved that."

"Maybe he did. I heard he murdered someone. Maybe the gods are evening out the score. Maybe it was retribution for a crime he committed."

"Stop talking nonsense," Myrrine says sharply. "Bad enough that your uncle is down there with his friends laughing and carrying on as if he's celebrating the poor man's death. It's indecent. Dangerous too."

"What do you mean?" I ask, suddenly uneasy.

"The man was murdered. There will be an inquiry. Unless they have a suspect already, they'll ask who would have benefitted from his death. Your uncle owed him money. That's bound to look suspicious."

"But he wouldn't have—" I protest.

"Are you so sure of that? Doesn't it strike you as odd that a man should just happen to be murdered on the day he was to bring his new bride home?"

When she puts it like that, I have to admit it does look odd. But I doubt my uncle had anything to do with the death of Euphrastus. After all, he had no qualms about marrying me to the man to repay his gambling debt. Then another thought strikes me. Maybe it's my fault. I prayed to Athena to save me from such a marriage. Could it be that the warrior goddess answered my prayer? A shiver runs through me. But Euphrastus did not die on a battlefield, I tell myself. He was struck down in his own home. Surely that is not the sort of death Athena would have meted out. Then I remember that the goddess isn't the only one I turned to for help. I also turned to Aspasia. Is it possible she arranged for the death of Euphrastus? The last time I saw her she told me she could do nothing, but maybe she did after all. As the mistress of Pericles, she must have many connections. How hard would it have been for her to arrange the death of a man like Euphrastus? Does Aspasia have that kind of power? I'm not sure.

Maybe Maron would know. I'll have to ask him. I can't wait to tell him what happened. I'll go look for him first thing tomorrow. He'll probably be on the Acropolis at work on the frieze at the little temple of Athena Nike. I can just imagine the look of surprise on his face when he sees me. I'll need a chaperone of course. Maybe I can persuade Myrrine to go with me. But if I can't, I'll just have to sneak out and go on my own.

That night after all the excitement, I don't think I'll sleep a wink, but then I fall asleep almost as soon as my head touches my pillow. The day has been more exhausting than I realized. It's still dark when a light hand on my shoulder wakes me.

"Get up," Myrrine whispers in my ear, "and make no noise."

"What is it?" I ask.

"Shh. Someone will hear you."

With clumsy fingers I tie my belt around my waist. Myrrine hands me my mantle.

"We're going out?" I ask, perplexed. "In the middle of the night?"

"Don't ask so many questions," she says impatiently.

I don't understand why we're getting up in the night. Why is she being so mysterious?

"Now don't make a sound," she warns again at the top of the stairs. "If your uncle wakes, we're all going to be in trouble."

After all the wine he drank at the wedding feast, I think it will take the war cries of an advancing army to wake him, but I keep that to myself and tiptoe down the stairs behind her. To my surprise, Kalchas is waiting at the foot of the stairs. He puts a warning finger to his lips, and since he isn't someone to trifle with even in normal circumstances, I don't ask again what it's all about.

We glide toward the door as silent as shadows. Kalchas opens it and one by one we slip out into the night. Once we are outside, he picks up a torch already lit and waiting by the door and motions for us to follow him. I see then that someone is waiting in the street for us—a small figure in a mantle.

"Chloe!" I exclaim in surprise when the torchlight falls on her face.

"Keep your voice down," Kalchas growls, eyes darting about.

"What's this about?" I ask Chloe in a low voice.

"It's Maron," Myrrine says before Chloe has time to answer.

"What about Maron?"

"He's in trouble," Chloe says. "You've got to help him, Rhea."

I'm wide awake now, but I still don't understand. "What do you mean? What kind of trouble?"

"They think he killed Euphrastus." She lays a hand on my arm.

"But that's impossible. Maron wouldn't do something like that." The words are hardly out of my mouth when I remember how he threatened Euphrastus with his knife that night we went to his house. Would he have killed Euphrastus to keep me from having to marry him? Was he capable of violence like that? Surely not.

"There must be some mistake," I say, looking from Chloe to Myrrine and from Myrrine to Kalchas.

"They're searching for him even now," Chloe says.

"Who is?"

"The Scythian guard. We have to hurry. If they find him, it will be too late."

"You know where he is?"

"Yes, I'll take you there."

Kalchas gives Myrrine a quick kiss and murmurs something in her ear too low for me to hear. Evidently they don't care if I see. It's as if all the rules have changed. Under my mantle I'm shivering. This can't be happening. Maron would never kill anyone. It must all be a misunderstanding.

"Be careful," Myrrine whispers as she clings to Kalchas. He nods.

Then we start down the street, Kalchas in the lead with the torch, followed by Chloe and me. When I look back, Myrrine is still standing by the door, watching us.

CHAPTER 30

The full moon shines down on the street and the houses, bathing everything in a ghostly light. Gradually Chloe explains what happened. The Scythian archers showed up at the house where Maron lodges with fellow sculptors and artisans and demanded to see him. While others kept the archers talking, he climbed from a courtyard balcony on the second floor onto the tiled roof. From there he leapt to a lower roof and then to the ground and took off running. He had overheard enough to know they thought he had murdered Euphrastus. In the case of a slave accused of murdering a citizen, the slave is at a disadvantage. He would most probably be imprisoned or executed when they found him. He was concerned I might never know what happened to him, so he made his way through the streets of the Ceramicus to the house of Chloe's music teacher. He knew where she lived because he had asked someone after I ran into him in the Ceramicus that day.

When he pounded on the door, the music teacher refused to let him talk to Chloe, but the noise attracted the attention of everyone in the house, including Chloe and Nessa. As soon as the excitement died down, Chloe slipped out and found him hiding in the shadows. He told her what had happened and begged her to take a message to me. He wanted to see me one last time, but he was afraid if he went to our house my uncle would turn him over to the Scythian archers. Although Chloe had never met Maron before, she was struck by the romance and danger of the situation and promptly agreed to help him. Her employment as a flute girl at banquets frequently required her to be out and about at night, so she had no qualms about crossing the city in the dark alone.

As we near the agora, we stop talking because now there are revelers in the streets on their way home from a banquet or on their way to the next one. Chloe and I keep our faces hidden by our mantles. Some of the revelers call out to us, inviting us to join them. Kalchas stares straight ahead and we keep walking.

Maron has taken shelter at the Altar of the Twelve Gods, a roofless rectangular walled enclosure of stone in the agora with an altar in the center. Within its walls anyone claiming sanctuary is under the protection of the twelve gods. While Maron is there, he can't be harmed. Nevertheless, he tried to hide himself by crouching in a corner. When we enter the sanctuary, he springs up and crosses the distance between us in a few strides.

"You came." He stares at me as if he is trying to memorize my face.

"Of course I came." I look around, frightened for him of the danger he is in. What will happen when the Scythian archers find him? Shouldn't he be better hidden?

Kalchas stations himself by the open doorway, scrutinizing the agora through narrowed eyes. Chloe stands watch at the gap in the back wall.

"Do you think anyone followed you?" Maron asks Kalchas over his shoulder.

"I don't think so," Kalchas says.

"You didn't kill Euphrastus, did you?" I ask anxiously.

"Of course not. But the archers say they have a witness who saw me threaten him."

Kalchas turns his head at that. "A witness?"

"It's my fault," I hasten to explain. "We went to his house to talk to him. Maron was just defending me."

"It won't matter," Kalchas says, scowling. "Not if there was a witness."

"But Maron is innocent. You heard him. He didn't kill Euphrastus."

Kalchas glances at us. "He's a slave. Who will believe him? And if you explain why you were there, your reputation will be ruined."

"I don't care about my reputation."

"You will if you lose it."

"He's right," Maron says before I can argue. "You have to stay out of this, Rhea."

"What will they do to you?" I ask, biting my lip.

"I expect they'll send me to the silver mines at Laurium." His voice is flat, emotionless.

The silver mines are the equivalent of a death sentence.

We both know that. Men seldom last more than six months in the mines.

"No, you can't go."

"I won't have a choice."

I refuse to accept that. "Run away. Don't let them catch you."

There is sadness in his eyes. He runs a finger down my cheek. "There's no place in the city they can't find me. You know that."

"Then leave the city."

"That's not so easily done when you're a fugitive from justice."

"You can't just give up! Kalchas, tell him."

"I have no choice."

"You do," I say fiercely. "You asked me to run away with you. All right. Let's run away together."

"No, I have nothing to offer you now. I can't ask you to share that kind of burden."

"It's my choice. We'll go together."

"You'd regret it. You said yourself that you can't leave Athens."

I look straight into his eyes. "I've changed my mind. I want to be with you." And it's true. I don't know why I didn't understand this earlier. Why was I so smitten by Doros that I didn't see how much Maron loved me? No, I had seen it. It was my own feelings I was blind to, my own heart I was ignorant of. Have I come to my senses too late?

"If you're going to run away," Kalchas says from the doorway, "you should do it soon. Once the sun comes up, it won't be long before the Scythian archers find you. If you leave now, you may be able to make it to the Long Walls."

"I have no money with me," Maron says. "I won't be able to get passage on a ship."

"If you stay here, you'll die. And it's too dangerous to go back to your lodgings."

Maron looks down at me and tucks a loose lock of hair behind my ear. The touch of his fingers brushing against my cheek sends a shiver through me. "You can't come," he says again. "I want you to. You can't imagine how much I want you to. But I can't ask that of you."

"I'm going with you," I say, determined now. My mind is made up and he's not going to change it. What do I have to stay in Athens for?

"You're not used to hardship," he argues. "You have no idea what it's like to be cold or hungry. All your life you've been sheltered."

He may be uncertain, but I'm not. "If I stay here, I'll have to marry a man my uncle chooses," I remind him, "maybe even my uncle himself. That's if I don't die of plague first or the Spartans don't conquer the city and enslave us all. I prefer to take my chances with you. I prefer to be with a man I choose."

He hesitates, his brow furrowed, torn between my offer and his conscience. "But I'll be a hunted man, a runaway slave."

"I don't care. Let me go with you. I want to be where you are."

He pulls me close and kisses me. It feels good and right to have his arms around me. I don't ever want him to let me go.

"There will be time for that later," growls Kalchas. "Now go."

I rush to Chloe, keeping watch at the gap in the back wall, and hug her. She presses an obol into my palm. "You need this more than me."

Looking down at it, I wonder if it's the same obol I gave her that day in the marketplace. It was only a few weeks ago, but how circumstances have changed since then!

"I'll miss you," I tell her.

She arranges my mantle over my head. "May the gods go with you," she says softly.

CHAPTER 31

Maron holds my hand as we hurry through the nearly deserted streets with only the light of the moon to guide us. We don't talk. With so much at stake, we have to stay alert. At any moment a cry might ring out if we are discovered. We stay on narrow backstreets as much as possible as we make our way from the agora to the Piraeus gate. This gate, unlike the other gates of Athens which lead out of the city, opens onto a walled road that leads to Athens' port at Piraeus. The Long Walls were built after the Persians sacked our city to ensure that Athens would not be cut off from supplies if it were ever under siege again by an enemy, as it is now by the Spartans and their allies. Broad enough for two oxen-drawn wagons to pass each other, it's crowded with makeshift hovels in which refugees from the countryside have found shelter. On either side of the road rise the high walls that run the four and a half miles to Piraeus.

I have never before walked between the Long Walls. It's a little like walking through a tunnel although the night sky is overhead. Above us from time to time we can see the sentinels on watch atop the outer wall, black shadows against the sky. It's darker here than in the city because the walls block out the moonlight. We keep in the narrow open path between the refugees encamped on either side. Eyes follow us, dogs bark, children wake and cry. I keep close to Maron and try to hide my fear. There may be thieves among them who would attack us for the clothes on our backs. I hope he still has the knife he had the night we went to confront Euphrastus.

Maron wants to reach the safety of Piraeus before the sun comes up, so we keep walking even though we're tired. I can scarcely believe I had the courage to run away with him and cast my lot with his. I wonder what my uncle will say when he finds me gone. Maybe he will be relieved. He will be able to claim the property left behind by my parents. I'm sorry I didn't have a chance to say good-bye to Nikomedes, but I think he will understand. Chloe will explain to him what happened. Maybe someday we'll meet again and catch up on all that happened since we parted. I hope I'll see Myrrine and Kalchas again someday too. I try not to think about the little plot in the cemetery outside the Dipylon Gate where my family lie buried. Surely they too would understand. There is nothing else I regret leaving behind except my scrolls.

"What are you thinking so hard about?" Maron asks after we have walked along for some time in silence. "Having second thoughts?"

I shake my head. "No, I was thinking about my scrolls."

"We'll buy more," he promises, squeezing my hand. "Poetry for you and a hammer and chisel for me."

I smile up at him. I don't really care about the scrolls. I just don't want him to be captured by the Scythian archers. We walk for a while again in silence. My thoughts turn to the mysterious death of Euphrastus.

"Do you think Aspasia arranged for his murder?" I ask him.

"Why would you think that? I've never heard her spoken of as a cruel woman. There are many who are jealous of her, but everyone praises her intelligence and beauty."

"She said she would help me."

"I doubt she meant by killing him."

I glance up at Maron. "Then you think it was thieves?"

"More likely it was that slave, the woman who answered the door the night we went there."

"Why do you think it was her?"

"Do you remember the bruise on her face?"

I nod. I see her as clearly in my mind as if she were standing before us.

"Think about it. Why else was she so quick to tell the Scythian archers about me? And who else knew I had threatened him? It was an easy way for her to deflect blame. She rid herself of an abusive master and escaped punishment for the deed. Who knows, maybe she got the idea when we showed up on his doorstep. Stabbing him on the day of the marriage made it look as if I were to blame. It was a neat plan. She's a clever woman."

"I'm sure he deserved it, but you shouldn't have to pay the penalty for her crime."

"It's not a just world. Haven't you figured that out? And besides she saved us both from lives we didn't want."

"Me, yes," I agree, "but were you so unhappy working on your friezes?"

"I might have gone on like that for a long time, grumbling at my lot but not dissatisfied enough to change it. She did me a favor giving me a reason to leave."

"But your friezes—"

"I don't have to stay in Athens to be a sculptor."

I hope he's right. He seems more confident about going into exile than I am. I'm not sure what awaits us once we have turned our backs on the civilized world. But at least we will be together.

Dawn is breaking when we finally emerge from the tunnel of the Long Walls and get our first glimpse of Piraeus. It sprawls before us, a jumble of sunbaked buildings clinging precariously to the hillside and stretching as far as the eye can see. I'm astonished that the harbor city is so large. It looks nearly as large as Athens but without her splendid architecture and impressive monuments. As we wander through the crowded streets, I feel as if I'm in a foreign city because all around us we hear foreign tongues. Maron, who has been in Piraeus before, is amused at my astonishment at everything I see. We spend the obol on some figs at a stall in the marketplace. Then he takes us to a quarter of the city with which he is familiar where we can search for lodgings. Although we have no money, he haggles with a landlady and secures a room with the promise to pay her in a day or two.

Maron knows where work is to be found. Leaving me in

our lodgings, he spends the first day at the docks helping unload corn from a ship. He comes home tired and sweaty, but he grins when he pulls out the drachma he has earned for his labor. For a while this becomes the pattern of our days.

I don't like sitting about while he's out working and I'm bored. My only diversion is watching from our balcony as the landlady's children play in the courtyard below. She has a boy of seven and a girl of five. She's always scolding them and bemoaning their unruliness. On impulse I offer to watch them.

"But I have no money to pay you," she protests.

"It's all right," I assure her. "You don't need to pay me."

"It's a shame the boy is not in school," she says with a sigh, "but I can't afford it. He'll end up a common laborer, I suppose. But such is life. I'm a poor widow. What can I do?"

"If you like, I can teach him how to read," I offer. "The girl too."

"Can you do that?" she asks eagerly, her eyes lighting up. She glances over at her children. "But you don't need to teach the girl. Reading is useless for girls."

"The world is changing," I tell her. "Perhaps one day she too will be a poor widow."

The woman eyes me narrowly, and for a moment I fear I've offended her. Then she sighs again. "Perhaps it wouldn't hurt to teach the girl too. And perhaps I could charge you a little less for your lodgings in return."

So our deal is struck and in the days that follow I give lessons to her children.

But we know that we can't stay indefinitely in Piraeus.

It's easy to think that we blend in and no one will notice us, but always hanging over us is the fear that we may be caught.

We save aside what we can of Maron's meager wages, and he quietly inquires about passage on the cargo ships that dock in the harbor. One day he finds a ship bound for Syracuse which will take us on. A sprawling port city on the island of Sicily, it seems as good a destination as any other. We'll be safely out of reach of the Scythian archers but not totally beyond the reach of civilization.

And so one day in early spring when leaves are starting to sprout on the olive trees, we board a ship carrying pottery and olive oil and set sail for our new life. As I stand on deck, I look back with tears in my eyes at the land that has been the only home I have ever known. I have no idea when I'll see it again, if ever, or how much it will change or how much I'll change. Maron puts his arm around me. It feels strong and comforting. Then I turn and look the other way at the open sea and the unknown future that lies before us.

AUTHOR'S NOTE

The Peloponnesian War — the war fought between Athens and Sparta and its allies — lasted twenty-seven years, ending in 404 B.C. with the defeat of Athens. It marked the end of the golden age of Ancient Greece, the period which had witnessed the creation of many beautiful buildings like the Parthenon for which we remember the Ancient Greeks today. The golden age saw the flourishing of Greek theatre, philosophy, art, and architecture. Athens would never again reach the heights it reached during that period.

The plague which struck Athens in several waves beginning in the second year of the war decimated the population, causing the city to lose one-third or more of its population (estimates vary). The increased number of people sheltering in the city as a result of the siege no doubt contributed to the conditions which made the plague so deadly.

Syracuse, the city in Sicily to which Maron and Rhea flee, was attacked by an expedition of Athenian warships in 415 B.C., but with the help of a Spartan general Syracuse prevailed. The decision to attack Syracuse ultimately proved disastrous for Athens since it lost two hundred ships and thousands of men. The conflict with Syracuse is considered the turning point in the Peloponnesian War which led to the defeat of Athens.

When the war was over, some of Sparta's allies called for the destruction of Athens and the enslavement of its people, but Sparta chose to be merciful. The long and costly war, however, resulted in Athens' loss of influence and power and was a blow from which it would never fully recover.

I relied on many sources during the writing of this novel and tried to be true to the known historical facts of the period, although at times I encountered disagreement among my sources. In particular there was disagreement regarding the lives of women. That women did not have equality with men seems evident (they could not hold office or vote), but I found it harder to agree with historians who suggested women seldom left their homes except to participate in festivals. Plays from the period such as *Antigone*, *Medea*, and *Lysistrata* suggest that there were strong women in the society. Even the fame and respect accorded Aspasia challenges the notion that women lived shadow lives. So I hope historians will overlook any liberties I have taken in my portrayal of a young woman coming of age during the early years of the Peloponnesian War.

ABOUT THE AUTHOR

Deanna Madden has taught literature and creative writing at colleges on the U.S. mainland and in Hawaii. Her publications include short stories, essays on literature, the novella *The Haunted Garden*, and the novels *Helena Landless*, *Gaslight and Fog*, *The Wall*, and *Forbidden Places*. She lives in Honolulu with her family and is at work on her next novel.